DESTINY'S JOURNEY

LADY BEE

DEDICATION

I dedicate this book to my only child, my daughter Amber.
Twenty-two years ago, when the dream of writing this book came about,
I became a mom for the first time. I guess something had to take the back
seat and it wasn't going to be you. Between catering to your every need as a
mother and standing behind you through the years, watching you grow, my
dream of writing this book was on the back burner, simmering.
To the evenings you saw me writing and wondered why, to the times
you pointed out to friends and family that your mom would write on any
and everything, and then there was my constant observation of people and
things that I shared with you and was met with silence. I know you
wondered about me. I know you wondered why I couldn't just be your
mom, just read a book instead of obsessing about writing one.
Well, I couldn't, because I had a dream that needed to be fulfilled, my
novel Destiny's Journey.
Sweetheart, I'm dedicating this novel to you and hope that one day
when you open the pages and begin to read it you will understand why.
I LOVE YOU. Mum.

ACKNOWLEDMENTS

I want to thank my creator for allowing me a place on this earth, for believing in me when no one else did, for opening my eyes to your love and truth and for entrusting me with a dream that I now know was not too big to be fulfilled.

Thanks for the strength, the courage and the belief that you have instilled in me all these years. Thank you for making me brave enough, to step forward when you called me. Thank you for choosing me.

Thanks to my support team, who never wavered, who came together and worked along with me side by side the last couple of months. After two years of hard work I delivered a manuscript to my editor Delana Isles, asking her to help me bring my manuscript from the first draft to a more refined stage and then to publishing. I was drawn to your quiet strength and warm spirit and when you said, "Let's do it" little did I know how tirelessly you would work on my little book and preserve that dream of mine in such a classy way. I want to thank you for believing in me and my work enough and never showing a moment of doubt. You set out to trim the corners, connect the dots and smooth out humps, making my story flow well enough to be published. Thanks for keeping the faith and for delivering like a pro. Your dedication to me and my novel was more than I could ask for. Thank you for showing up and being that angel that I needed to believe in me and to guide me on this journey. I am forever grateful for you, thank you.

I wish to acknowledge Michael Fenimore, from FENIMORE GRAPHICS who designed my book cover. You listened kindly to my vision of what I wanted my book cover to convey, even without reading my manuscript. Thanks for capturing my words and my image and putting them together to form my vision in picture, in the most artistic way. Your attention to detail, your discipline and dedication did not go unnoticed, right down to the day of publishing. Thanks for being on my team and following me on my journey.

I would also like to acknowledge my sisters: Yvette, Onemia, Heartlyn, Sivilene, Donna and Yvonne. I know you all have stood behind and beside me, rolling your eyes at times, wishing I would shut up about writing this book. You wondered why I thought it was possible, even though some of you still encouraged me by giving me pens and stationaries as gifts, spurring me on to my dreams, knowing that nothing was going to stop me. I sincerely believe that we all come into this life to fulfill a purpose, and I guess this was mine, or at least part of. Well, I did it and I want to say thanks to you guys for the encouragement and the silent thoughts of, "What if she actually did it?"

I hope I put smiles on your faces when you read it, I also hope you know that you were all a big part of this journey of mine. Thank you for listening and for your endless sisterly love.

PROLOGUE

Dad, I am going to London with you and Destiny next week. Lily had two reasons to be in London and she hoped her dad was not going to ask her why. She had contemplated bulldozing any objections, firmly stating that she was going to London with him and Destiny, like it or not, but as she stared at his bent head in front of her, the last four words got stuck in her throat.

She knew she would be pushing it too far had she added those four words, but she was determined to go as she had begun to notice that something was changing with her dad and she was not sure she liked what those changes indicated.

Lily had just finished up a five-minute meeting with him in his office. She had stood up and was about to leave as her dad got busy on his computer again.

But, girding her courage, she decided to jump right in, ready to do battle if he even thought of arguing with her after she blurted out the words. Hands on his desk, she leaned in waiting for him to look up at her, smile, then cave in to her demands like he's done so many times before. After all that is what he loved about her - her ability to get what she wanted without pleading, so much like his own strong-willed personality.

But just in case he did say no, she had a plan B. She had thought of a few questions he might ask and had prepared her answers to sway him to her way of thinking, but she was hoping it would not come to that and run the risk of him finding out the truth. So, she stood there waiting for that one word - okay.

She reasoned that he could not possibly say no to her demands as she would be taking over the firm very soon and asking to share a last business trip with him as a final learning experience could not raise any red flags.

Of course, her going to London alone with their client would be the better option; it would certainly make what she had planned so much easier to accomplish. But an opportunity existed right now as her dad was busy and she knew there was no better time to pitch her idea. She was hoping he would be so distracted he would hastily say okay to her idea.

Daniel looked up from his paperwork to see his daughter still standing there, leaning over his desk, only just realizing what she had said. He sighed, thinking that their meeting was over, and he would have to be firm that his decision about London was final. After all, she was needed here now that John Cramer, the other senior partner was away. If she went to London with him then all three senior partners would be absent from the firm and he did not want his law firm to be left in the hands of associates for the next week.

She ought to know that this was not the way to get to him. These tactics may have worked on him when she was five years old, but at thirty-five he was well aware of her ploys. What has gotten into her? He belatedly wondered if his beautiful, well-educated daughter was becoming like him in her tenacity.

He sighed, thinking that being a lawyer suited her too well, as she knew all the tricks of the trade and never failed to employ them to get what she wanted out of people. However, today he was determined to shut her out. "Lily," he said, looking up from his computer and into those green eyes of hers. "Let's stick to the topic at hand." He paused, hoping she would agree yet knowing even if she did she would not mean it, so he continued.

"Right now, I am sending an email to Camelot to advise them of the date we will be arriving in London and to schedule an appointment with them. When they confirm the appointment, I want you to ask them what documents we have to bring with us. Also, ask them to kindly fax us a copy of the claim form for Destiny Johnson to fill in before we get there and please make a note that I need to meet with the accountant tomorrow morning.

"Please get me a few copies of the company formation forms for that meeting at 9:00 am, we will be meeting with Ms. Johnson at 4:00pm today. We, meaning you and I, okay. That's all Lily, I have to get back to work now."

Lily said okay and backed away from her father's desk. She had not gotten a direct answer to her demands, but she was not about to give up. She wondered if her dad was developing romantic feelings for his new client, thinking that would be a very bad idea if that were the case.

She looked back at her dad before leaving his office and she noticed it then - he was different, he looked happy and ready to seize the moment.

She had not seen him like that since her mom died. She felt frozen in place as this realization hit her, only becoming aware that she hadn't moved until he looked up from his desk and asked if there was a problem. Shaking off the feeling that had suddenly overcome her, she smiled reassuringly at him, not wanting to lie, then tried to make her legs move before her mouth could. That's when she saw what she couldn't readily identify before - her dad was well groomed, and he looked ten years younger.

That thought kicked her legs into overdrive, propelling her hurriedly out of his office before impulsive words could escape her mouth. As the door clicked shut behind her, she leaned against it, closing her eyes and taking a deep breath. She felt a deep urge to go back inside and confront him with her suspicions.

Oh My God, she thought aghast, he really does have a crush on his new client. She recalled how tipsy he appeared the other night when she picked him up in front of the restaurant where he had just had dinner with Ms. Johnson, and how he could not stop singing her praises when he got into the car. She had dismissed it as the alcohol talking and did not make an issue of it because he had just signed on a new client, but looking at him just now, well-groomed and glowing with suppressed excitement, there was definitely something going on and she felt this was reason to be concerned.

Since when did he care how he looked anymore?

Lily thought that Ms. Johnson was too young for her dad, and besides, she probably has zero interest in him beyond a lawyer client relationship. My God! Dad is sixty-four years old. What is he thinking?

Now she had more than his drinking to worry about and she was determined to be on that flight to London with him and Ms. Johnson. End of discussion.

I WON!!

It was taking a while for my brain to catch up to my eyes.
I was alone, and I soon realized that this was way too big to be contained so I let out a scream, "Yes, yes, I won!"
I walked away from my computer, circled the couch, the loveseat, then the chairs in my living room. I wanted to tell somebody, but I was still trying to absorb it myself. Calm down Destiny, I told myself, calm down.

My heart was racing as I paced the floor, wild thoughts flying through my head - Omg! Omg! Holy shit I won, yes, I won finally! Oh God, oh God I am going to have a heart attack. I sat down on the couch, ticket in hand, shaking, trying to pull myself together but I just couldn't. Shit, I won the lottery. I won the lottery, I kept exclaiming to myself.

All six of my numbers were illuminated on the computer screen and I recognized them without looking at my ticket. Those six numbers that I had played for years had finally come in and I had just won ten million dollars! Thank you, Thank you. My dream has finally come true, but it was no longer a dream, it was real, oh my god, thank you, it's real.

At that moment I began shaking like a leaf in the wind, trying to make sense of what I was seeing. It really was not as simple as I thought it would be. I felt light headed, like I was going to lose consciousness. Almost of its own volition my body slid into the couch. I squeezed its arm – reassurance - I desperately needed it. I closed my eyes, trying as hard as I could to calm down. Come on Destiny, breathe in, breathe out, slowly, again, breathe in, breathe out. As my heart rate slowed down, I began to cry. Not the dainty, sniffling kind of ladylike cry, I balled.

I had been playing lotteries for over twenty years and had never won anything.

I started playing the UK lottery a few months ago and now here I am, already a big winner. How am I going to sleep tonight? Why did I decide to check my ticket numbers? I could have done so in the morning. It was almost 9:00pm on a Sunday night when I decided to check.

I had wondered if it was necessary, if I really needed to do this tonight as it was just one hour away from my bedtime, but I had this burning desire to check the UK lottery site to see the numbers that had come in yesterday. It was almost like the universe was speaking to me, telling me that I needed to know tonight, this could not wait.

Now here I am with all these emotions rushing through my body and I'm unable to cope.

I looked over at my computer from where I was sitting on the couch and I could still see the numbers on the screen. I knew those numbers by heart, they were so personal to me, each one representing an important date in my life. I closed my eyes and repeated them one by one, all six of them. I couldn't believe this, it had actually happened after all these years. I struggled out of the couch and onto shaky legs, sat down at my computer again, wiping away the tears streaming down my face, trying to focus.

Dear God, an answer to a prayer! Thank you. I had literally just won ten million dollars. What am I going to do now? I am too scattered brained right now to carry on a conversation, so maybe I should send a group email to my sisters. That thought only held for thirty - seconds before my brain clicked on and eliminated it, Not now. I needed more time to wrap my head around the fact that this has really happened, so I turned off my phone and went to bed.

I laid there as a myriad of thoughts swirled throughout my head, none getting a firm foothold in my consciousness. I was hoping that at any given moment my brain would tire from the unexpected stimuli and would shut down, allowing me to fall asleep, but with each passing hour my eyes got brighter. The thought that I needed to share this information with someone I can trust persisted, pestering me and chasing away all glimmer of sleep.

I knew that I needed to calm down and relax in order to sleep, so I decided to watch a movie. One movie led to another yet sleep evaded me as I continued to chant thanks to God for answering my prayers.

It was 6am Monday and I was still wide awake.

I could not distract myself enough to fall asleep, so I took a sleeping pill and waited. I finally fell asleep around 10am and woke up around the same time the next day. On waking, there was an immediate feeling that a momentous shift had occurred in my life. I was finally a winner.

I had needed two days to truly absorb it; this was so different, oh my god, everything was different now.

Where did I put my ticket? I anxiously got out of bed to make sure I had put it in a safe place and that my name was still written on the back of it. Why that would change, I don't know, but this is where I am now, this is my life.

After having a small bowl of cereal for breakfast I poured myself a cup of freshly brewed coffee. Gazing curiously into the coffee, I wondered if this too would taste different. I have been drinking the same brand of coffee for several years, but now would be a good time to change it.

My life lately seems like a continuously rolling hamster wheel of change. I am experiencing an empty nest and a marital separation, both in the same year. Now this, winning the lottery, a change like no other. I recalled Sunday morning when I woke up feeling like the day was different from any other in the past month.

I was just beginning to feel better after the storm had swept through my life five months ago, and that morning I felt better than I had on my birthday. That was the day I was brave enough to orally express what I'd been feeling for the last four years - I no longer wanted to be married. That decision came with its own set of discomforts that left me wondering if I'd made the right choice, but on Sunday morning, as I laid in bed, the same side I have slept on for fifteen years of marriage and felt complete bliss, I felt alone, but not lonely. That mystical sense of peace you hear about from some separated and divorced people, had finally arrived.

I wanted to savor that feeling, eyes closed, and let whatever it was that had entered my room and taken over my body and mind to know that it was okay. So, I did just that. I closed my eyes and whispered, thank you for this, unaware of the changes that Saturday night had wrought while I slept. My Sunday morning bliss was the universe's way of telling me that my whole world had changed, my prayer had been answered.

But I am still getting used to my newfound freedom. It has taken me a while to admit this and as much as I had wanted it – it did take some adjusting to.

Like now, me driving to the gym on my own, I used to envision this, not having someone in my car critiquing everything I did while driving. Now I can drive the way I want, change lanes when I want and signal when I damn well please.

Oh, this feels good.

This is my new freedom and I am finally getting so comfortable with it that I'd forgotten to turn on my phone this morning. How do I handle this? My brain felt like it would jackhammer its way out of my head any time soon.

I parked the car and turned on my phone - so many messages and missed calls, three from my daughter Anna who had spent the week at her friend's house.

She was coming home today and probably needed me to pick her up, or maybe she just wanted to say good morning to her mom. Boy, if she only knew what has happened to me, but I won't say, not yet, I will simply reply to all of them saying Happy Tuesday Morning. The word Happy would say it all. It implies that all is well. I am happy, yes, I certainly am, in ways, they would never imagine.

The smile that came to my face was more than enough to say what I was feeling and my fingers on the phone wanted to spell it out in big bold letters - Happy Tuesday Morning ladies, guess what I won ten million dollars in the lottery!

Yes, I could send a group message to all of them at once, making their Tuesday almost as exciting as mine. I just wanted to share my joy with my loved ones before I went in and burned off some calories. The moment was too big not to share. So, I began typing to my friends and family.

I kept the message simple enough that they would be as shocked as I was at first, rather than happily surprised and start calling me back. Am I sure about this? My phone will never stop ringing and my mouth would soon be dry from the constant chatter from the calls congratulating me on my win followed by the never-ending questions: When did this happen? Where did this happen? How did this happen?

The suggestions of what I could do with all that money and how they wish it had happened to them, then the thinly veiled hints about a new car, being able to take a vacation for once in their life, wishes that they had a little more money tucked away so they can retire earlier, or finally own a home or finish paying for the one they have. I knew it would all tug at my heartstrings, and that they would take this opportunity to make themselves deserving of it. This is exactly what would happen.

I would be asked to make promises that I would forget I'd made or simply wished I hadn't but did, because I was so caught up in the moment. I knew that years later I would regret it. Looking down at my phone and the words I had typed, my gut was screaming no, you are going to regret this, say nothing for now.

I saw it - the jealousy, hatred, animosity and broken relationships this happy Tuesday can bring, friendships will be strained, even lost, and love can become hate. I could see it, see the other side of my winning, my joy could just as easily become my pain. Yes, I want to share this, but not now, I needed sound advice from a professional on what my first move should be. I needed time, more time to figure things out.

I held down the delete button on my phone and watched those extra words disappear and all that was left was 'Happy Tuesday, Morning all' then I hit send.

That was all I wanted to share for now.

ADJUSTING

I opened a bottle of Pinot Grigio and poured myself a glass to toast to a beautiful day before sitting down to a lunch of baked chicken, spinach salad and garlic bread.

I like to say that at my age eating light means longer life, I really love the way that rhymes. With every sip of wine, I thought of how lucky I was. I was slowly coming around to saying it without feeling strange, I'm rich.

I am still trying to imagine what that life would look like; how different it would be - rich and single.

Okay let's be honest here, I'm not exactly single as yet but that's only a matter of paperwork. There really is no going back, I had already moved on in my mind long before I said those words, I just needed to say them out loud and be true to myself. Our marriage had been over for years and we both knew it, we were just waiting for the other to say it.

I shook off those thoughts, that's behind me now. Right now, I was getting a taste of the freedom I had longed for, even though it was taking a bit of getting used to. This whole thing is so new to me, I'm not sure what to do next. Should I go on a cruise for a month or should I have a summer fling with a younger man? Which will be more fun? Which would cost me less money?

But that's the old Destiny speaking, money is no longer a problem. At this very moment, everything felt exhilarating and I needed to do something out of the ordinary.

I felt like any minute now I was going to break down with tears of joy, so I poured myself another glass of wine and went to lie down on the couch, still fantasizing about what I was going to do with my millions.

I became aware that a telephone was ringing in my ear. I looked down at the slim black object in my hand, wondering if I was doing the right thing. I started to hang up when my sister Heather answered at the other end with her customary chipper greeting, "Heeey child!"

Even with the phone inches away from my face, I heard her, and again wondered why her greeting always have to be so different from everyone else's. It matters not how many times I call her, her greeting always takes me by surprise and I'm usually left scrambling for a reply.

But today this was the least of my worries, as I'm now wondering if I'd called the right sister. Heather has always been unable to keep a secret, yet here I am about to share one with her. But I needed to share this with someone, so I jumped in, feet first.

"Heather, guess what!"

Usually she never guesses right, only responding with 'what', but today she surprised me, and she said, "You won the lottery." She nailed it. Sometimes it really seems like she can read my mind.

I paused, then blurted out yes, and she immediately started screaming in my ear, "I knew it! I knew it!"

A sense of relief overcame me, it felt like I had just transferred the anxiety I was carrying around for the last three days. She was so excited, she took over the conversation, barely allowing me to get in a word.

"I knew you would win one day," she said, "I always had a good feeling about you winning." Then she cut to the chase, "Sis, so how much did you win?"

"Hold on," I said, "let's take it from the top, shall we."

So, I sat there for the next ten minutes, the cool Caribbean breeze rifling through my hair, cooling my overheated skin and blowing the stress of the past 24 hours away with every word I uttered. It felt like my anxious energy was traveling from my condo, across the Atlantic Ocean to the USA where Heather lived. As I wrapped up my story, my sister corrected me, "You won ten million pounds girl, that's even more money, shut your mouth!"

Now she is hollering in my ear again and I'm forced to turn down the volume on the phone before I go deaf.

"I am so happy for you, sis. I am beyond proud of you right now," she kept saying, every word increasing in volume. Heather had always been a crier, and for the life of me I could never figure out where she stores all of that water. I knew I had to give her time to wrap her head around this before I dropped the rest on her.

This would probably be a good time to remove the phone from my ear and put her on speaker, she was giving me such a headache. Good god, she has some pipes on her. She knew I was going to give her some of the money, but how much she was not sure.

Still sniffing, she said, "Girl, if your husband finds out that you won ten million pounds he would be back for his half."

Damn, why did she had to go there, I was just beginning to feel good about calling her, but now I can feel the nervous energy returning. This would have been the right time to hang up on her, but first I had to make her swear to keep my secret.

"How is he going to find out?" I asked, "I won this in the UK, that's worlds away from here."

"I'm just saying, you need to get yourself a good lawyer, Destiny. I know you would still have a lot of money left even if you have to give up some to him and I know you are going to give your sister some of it too." She paused for a break and I immediately responded to both statements with," Of course, I would."

She started crying again and it did not sound pretty, yet the sound of her crying did not drown out the sound of my cellphone ringing next to me.

I jumped in fear, scrambling up from the couch and pushing the vibrating object away from my body and onto the floor.

I opened my eyes, startled, confused and a little disoriented, not even remembering closing them, or falling asleep. Whew! Thank God that was a dream.

I looked down at the phone, mind finally made up.

Time to get me a lawyer.

I wanted to share the news with my daughter Anna before I got a lawyer, but I knew she would not be able to keep it to herself.

It's hard for me to carry this around, so I can only imagine how hard it would be for her. She is so socially connected I think she would be sorely tempted to drop hints, or at least tell one of her friends who would then tell another friend and so on.

This is what the new generation do in cyberspace, bond with each other over shared information.

I sometimes believe that her friends know her better than I do, which I understand to an extent given that they are constantly communicating. I am no longer the first one she comes to for advice or an opinion. I have been reduced to the occasional chauffeur for her and her friends.

Clearly, my mom coolness has worn off now that she is nineteen and about to leave home. I supposed that in her own way she is becoming more independent and needed to show me that. This is what I have been wishing for a long time, her independence. Now here I am witnessing it firsthand.

She will be going off to university in a few months, living on campus far away from home and making new friends from different parts of the world.

I constantly hope that as she steps more and more into adulthood, she remembers those words of wisdom I shared with her and those teaching moments that she sometimes thought would never end.

Thankfully the eye rolling, the hissing, the door slamming and the shouting, all the things that drove me crazy, are now in the past. A new chapter of her life was beginning, and I just wanted her to be okay.

I smiled, imaging her sitting in the couch chatting away on her phone, clueless to the changes that were about to take over our lives and how nothing will ever be the same again. I consoled myself that while we are both starting new chapters in our lives, hopefully the changes will eventually bring us back together, maybe miles away from here, somewhere in Europe maybe.

I am still bursting with pride and joy and the one person I wished I could share it with is Anna, but I can't. This is a distraction that could eventually take her off course. Am I overthinking this? Maybe I should share this with her and watch my coolness come back.

I remember her telling me she could not keep a secret when she was eight years old, and now eleven years later since she's discovered social media telling her this would be like asking to be robbed.

I know she would be happy for me for about five minutes, get emotional then like a typical nineteen-year-old from the generation of entitlement she would start telling me how this could benefit her and how her life has now changed and that she just has to share this information with her friends.

I can see her now all over social media. Nope, I do not think so. I know the nature of my child and sadly I cannot share this with her right now.

Lawyer first, everyone else later.

AT THE LAW FIRM

I walked into the law firm of Daly Cramer & Shaw feeling like a million bucks.

No one at the firm knew that I had won the UK lottery or any lottery for that matter. A few days earlier I had made an appointment for a divorce consultation. I knew it was a lie, but what other choice did I have.

I could see what would have happened had I said I'd just won the lottery and I am looking for legal help. The lady answering the phone would be shaking her head in disbelief and thinking, oh yeah, she needs help alright, psycho. In my ear, I would hear the sound of her phone hitting the cradle when she hung up on me. No, I could not let that happen.

The pretty receptionist ushered me into Mr. Daly's office and told me that he would be in shortly. He had made the cut after I had eliminated three other lawyers from my list. I wanted an experienced older gentleman.

I know it probably sounds like a dating profile but if I wanted to date I would have chosen a younger man. I was looking for a lawyer. A lawyer who knew the English laws and whose only interest was making sure I was able to claim my money.

Up to this point I had no clue what Mr. Daly looked like, there were no photos of him. I'd read his bio and came up with a mental image of a sixty-four-year-old, overweight male, about five feet ten inches with salt and pepper hair, more salt than pepper. I was still trying to picture his face and while I had a few visuals I was finding them hard to accept. Maybe I wanted my lawyer to be handsome on some level.

I wanted to be wrong about the weight too, but I have witnessed many legal scholars sitting at the local bars knocking back a few beers at happy hour. The heat from the sun in this part of the world was reason enough to indulge, if only the after effects were not so brutal on their appearance. It seems as though these guys had not found the balance, which to me would be bar then gym, or vice versa.

Maybe I would have to settle for knowing that I'd chosen a brilliant legal mind. From my research I had learned that the founder of Daly, Cramer and Shaw, has been practicing law for over thirty years.

So, when he walked into the office three minutes later I was surprised how off the mark I was. Mr. Daniel Daly looked a bit like Harrison Ford in the face, about six feet tall with a pretty decent body for a man his age. That was the good part, but I still wondered if I had chosen wisely because the way he was dressed was not exactly impressive. Maybe I'm expecting too much because compared to him I'm feeling overdressed.

I know this is not a fashion show and his appearance should not matter that much, but it's so obvious, it's hard not to notice and wonder if maybe he did not want to come in to work today. He was making me question my choice.

He walked over to me, shook my hand and said, "Good morning, dear".

I thought he was going to call me darling, then I realized he probably did not know my name. I said, 'Nice to meet you Mr. Daly, I'm Destiny Johnson.

He quickly apologized and started over with, "A pleasure to meet you too, Ms. Johnson."

I watched him move away from me and sit behind his mahogany desk. He leaned back in his big black leather chair and I got a better look at my soon to be lawyer. He really did not have the polished look I was expecting, but maybe it was time I reeled in my expectations and reminded myself why I'm really here. But that became near impossible when he started yawing into his right hand. I tried my best to focus on something else, something more pleasing, but I could not get past the fact that he needed grooming. I wondered if he had a wife, or someone who loved him enough to say you cannot go into the office like this even if you are the boss.

He was still moving things around on his desk when his phone rang. Ignoring the ringing, he reached cross his desk to press a button, then looking straight at me he asked, "Ms. Johnson, what can I do for you?" Tapping on his desk with the pen as though he was counting down the seconds to my reply.

Not skipping a beat, I said, "Well Mr. Daly, I need your help because I just won ten million dollars in the lottery."

The tapping stopped abruptly, the pen clattered to his desk. He opened his mouth slightly as though he was going to say something, but no words came out. Obviously, he was having a hard time processing what I'd just said. This was certainly not what he was expecting to hear, was it? He was expecting me to talk about getting a divorce. He stared at me for what felt like an eternity, evaluating and assessing. Oh, how I wanted him to say something, anything.

I understood enough to know that lawyers don't want you rattling on, they like to ask the questions and you answer, just answer, they don't want an essay. Okay fine, maybe I sounded crazy to him, but crazy or not I needed a reply. It was his turn to speak.

His lips came together slightly, and he exhaled. He looked bothered, even a bit tired. He rubbed his hand over his face, opening his eyes wide as though he was trying to stay awake, no doubt wondering if I was just a figment of his tired brain.

Daniel shook his head to clear the cobwebs, did she just say she won ten million dollars? What is going on here? Damn, he really had drunk too much last night, he was not prepared for this. He held up his hand to signal to her to give him a few minutes, then reached for the phone on his desk. He asked for two cups of coffee with cream and sugar.

I was left wondering if he was suffering from a hangover or was it the curveball he was just served. I felt lost and a little stupid, but I took a little comfort in the fact that he had not laughed at me, although I'm not sure silence is significantly better. I guess he had never heard anyone say this to him before. On second thought, maybe the way I had just blurted it out was not the right way to go about this. My presentation needed work. That became clear when he hung up the phone and asked if he had understood me correctly.

"Did you just tell me that you won ten million dollars in the lottery?"

"Yes, Mr. Daly, that is exactly what I said."

"Okay," he said, "so you want me to…"

"I want you to claim my money for me," I promptly replied.

"I see," he said, yawning and blowing another hangover breath my way. I could see this was not going to be easy and I was not sure who was making less sense right now, him or me. I heard footsteps coming into his office, it was the coffee he had ordered. He offered me a cup. I shook my head, again wondering if I had made a mistake, he really did not appear as smart as I was hoping, and he was obviously hungover and still trying to sober up.

He began slowly stirring sugar into his coffee, clearly stalling for time, but my patience was running thin, so I began to speak. Maybe when I make everything clear he will finally wake up.

"Mr. Daly," I said, "I won ten million dollars in the UK lottery a week ago. There was just one winner and I am the sole owner of that ticket." Those green eyes of his opened wide under bushy eyebrows, he was hearing me all right. I continued, "And I have the ticket to prove it," as I reached into my purse for the ticket and handed it to him.

"I chose you to represent me because you are English, and you know the laws of your country. I want to hire you to claim my money for me. What I am saying Mr. Daly is that I would like for you to be my lawyer. Is that possible?"

Reading glasses perched near the tip of his nose, he looked down at the ticket in his hand, then back up at me. "Can you prove to me that this ticket belongs to you?"

"Yes, I can, I have the receipt of purchase. Here it is."

"Good, because I have a few questions that you would need to answer before we go any further. Having the receipt helps to answer a lot of them. Like where did you purchase it and when? Did you purchase it yourself or did someone purchase it for you? Sometimes these questions come up and if you can't answer them it can create a problem collecting."

He paused, "I have one more question, are you a citizen of the country?"

"Yes, I am. As I'm sure you already know, being a British Overseas Territory, Turks and Caicos Islands citizens have a right to British citizenship, residence in the UK and are allowed to play the national lottery"

"Good," he said, "very good. We are making progress."

"I hope you're not bothered by me asking you these questions, Ms. Johnson."

"Not at all," I said, in fact I was happy that he was finally present.

For the next several minutes I sat quietly as he explained how important this information was. He said these are questions I must have answers to if he was going to represent me and that having the ticket was one part of the equation, proving that it belongs to me was another, more important part.

"I don't want any surprises, Ms. Johnson," he said while scanning the ticket and shaking his head in what I could only guess was amazement.

Turning it over, he inspected the piece of paper as he brought it closer to his face. Placing it on his desk and pushing it off to one side, he nodded like he was pleased that his examination was foolproof and that I was indeed the real deal.

"I see you've signed it already. You are very smart," he said.

I felt so overwhelmed with emotion that I had finally made a breakthrough with him, I could not provide a response if he was looking for one. It has now been a week since I found out I had won the lottery, and I was still feeling like I would explode at any minute. I slowly exhaled, trying to calm myself.

"Do you know how many people forget to sign their tickets, Ms. Johnson," Mr. Daly asked, pointing to the back of the ticket.

I had no clue and I did not care, but I did not say that. I simply looked at him and made a noncommittal open-handed gesture. Honestly, I just wanted to move on, I had not come to his office for a lecture and by now I knew he was the brain in the room, that much was evident from his ego wall.

The entire wall to the right of desk was adorned with several framed certificates with the name Daniel P. Daly, law degrees and awards all showing recognition and accomplishment for work well done. This is why I needed him right now and hoped he would agree to take me on as a client. I knew he was smarter than me and even though I had just won ten million pounds we were not in the same league, this I understood.

Mr. Daly took off his reading glasses, leaned back in his chair and looked at me in silence for a few seconds. I stared back at him, hungry for words to fall from his lips. Say something please, I thought, this whole thing is so unnerving. He held the ticket up between two fingers, scanned it again with those deep green eyes of his and quietly said, "This is big, this is going to change your life."

Changing tactics unexpectedly he placed the ticket on his desk and asked if I would like another cup of coffee. I had not touched the cup that was placed in front of me even though I had declined it, so I said no.

He was waking up and did not appear as hungover, but he clearly still needed more caffeine, so I offered my untouched cup to him anything to keep him as present as he was right now.

He began writing down numbers from the front of the ticket, "Ms. Johnson, I need your permission to call Camelot to verify that you are indeed holding a winning ticket."

"You have my permission Mr. Daly, please go ahead and make that phone call."

He put the phone on speaker, and for the next three minutes I listened to words that will change my life forever. We were both smiling in the end.

My lottery ticket was confirmed by the Camelot Group in England as the only jackpot winning ticket sold for Saturday night's drawing. Things had just gotten real. I quietly said a quick prayer. Now it was time to hear welcome to the firm Destiny.

Mr. Daly got up from behind his desk and came over to me looking more aware of where he was now than he did ten minutes ago. He cracked a smile, shook his head and said, "Ms. Destiny Johnson, you have just hired yourself a lawyer. You are now my client and you can call me Dan."

We sealed the deal with a handshake and then I was overcome with emotions.

I said. "Thank you very much, but I cannot call you Dan."

Mr. Daly was still holding on to my hand, but in a comforting way now, he said, "Okay, then you can call me Daniel."

I was losing my composure and he saw it. The tears were welled up in my eyes and about to roll down my face, but I was not ready to let him see me cry so I got a hold of myself. Do not open the floodgates in his office I thought, that would be too embarrassing.

My lawyer looked at me concerned, not sure what to do, "Are you okay, Ms. Johnson?" Gently he let go of my hands, reached for a tissue and handed it to me. I am guessing that he has seen this before, so he knew what was coming.

I kept telling myself that you don't sit in your lawyer's office, cry after he agrees to take you on as a client and say it's okay to call him by his first name, but that is exactly what I did.

I thought of the night I found out that I had won, and I told him everything. How I wanted to tell someone but was too afraid to, until now. He was the only person I had told so far, and I trusted him to keep this information private until we claimed the money. He assured me that this was not a problem because I am now his client and that is part of the agreement.

He sat down next to me and held my hand again but this time he held it gently as he patiently watched me cry. It was such an emotional relief. I could not call my lawyer by his first name, but I did not know how to say that to him without looking silly. After a few more sniffles my tears dried up.

I was looking down at the mess I had made of myself when he calmly said, "Ms. Johnson, I want you to know that I am going to take good care of you. Don't you worry." He handed the lottery ticket back to me, telling me not to lose it. I promised him that would never happen, opened my purse and put it away.

My lawyer then said to me, "Ms. Johnson, you do know that in England they don't use dollars, so what you've actually won is ten million pounds, not ten million dollars."

I knew that, but I was not about to debate so I said in a surprised voice, "Oh, thanks for telling me." He then said he would have a contract drawn up and ready for me to sign on Monday.

"The contract will state that you have acquired this law firm to represent you. It will show our fees and the percentage we require as a retainer. Would you be accompanying me to London to claim your money or do you want us to claim it for you?"

"Which is cheaper?" I asked.

He looked at me in disbelief, "You've just won ten million pounds!"

"Well, now that you have reminded me, yes, I will be going to London with you."

I wanted to laugh, but my lawyer was all business, clearly ready to move on with his day. I stood up, purse in hand, ready to make my exit.

"Are there any more questions, Ms. Johnson?"

I had a laundry list of questions that I had only just started on. "Actually, I was hoping we could have the contract signed today," I replied. I knew I was pushing it, but I felt I had climbed up a notch on his client list.

"What about later on this evening? Is that possible?"

"Well, "I don't see why not, but once you've sign you are required to pay a retainer," he said. "Are you prepared to do that today?"

I reached into my purse and pulled out the lottery ticket, "This is my retainer. No, I will not be able to pay you today, but once you collect my money, I will pay your firm in full two percent of my winnings. You can put that in the contract."

The smile on his face said it all. "Put that ticket back in your purse, Ms. Johnson, I can see you came prepared. You must have done your homework."

"Is two percent enough?" I asked. We were both smiling now and before he could answer me I suggested dropping it to one and a half percent if I did not get that contract signed this afternoon.

"I have another client to see in half an hour, Ms. Johnson, and I am a bit pressed for time that is why I suggested we finalize this on Monday, but now that I see how determined you are, why not let me take my new client to dinner tomorrow night and we can sign the contract at the same time. How does that sound?"

"Mr. Daly are you asking me out?"

"No, Ms. Johnson, I am not asking you for a date. I am suggesting we have a business dinner to finalize your contract. I think you are going to be a valuable client to this firm."

I must say I liked hearing that, but not to appear too eager I said I would go to dinner on one condition.

"And what condition is that?" he asked.

Only if you are paying," I said.

He smiled, "Of course I'm paying, with pleasure. So, dinner tomorrow night at Turtle Bay restaurant, 8:00pm? Meet me there?" He was still holding my hand and waiting for confirmation from me. I had gotten a little lost in the warmth of his presence. Maybe I did want it to be a date.

"Turtle Bay restaurant at 8:00pm tomorrow," I said. "Yes, I will be there."

"Good, then I will see you tomorrow." Then he gently let go of my hand.

What the hell just happened? I couldn't explain it.

I left the law firm pleased that I had just hired a lawyer, but I now I needed to hire an accountant.

On my short drive home, I thought of where I wanted to keep my money. Should I bring my money to Turks and Caicos? If I did, in no time everyone would know, and my privacy would be gone.

In my country gossiping is like a national sport, people gossip about their enemies and their friends. But that's not the only thing that scares me. I am related to most islanders, and the place being so small, I know I would be hit upon constantly for handouts. It would never end, and I know it.

I want to give, I really do, but I want to give where it's really needed and will make an impact and change lives. Education has always been important to me and to start a scholarship foundation that can help children achieve higher education will warm my heart. Of course, the funds will be based on a commitment and a desire to go to university for four years and to acquire the knowledge that would not only help them, but years later help others.

I can see it now, those educated young leaders of tomorrow returning home, ready to give back to their community. Some of them are in Blue Hills spearheading our first Youth Center and Library. They are now equipped to help children living at the poverty level rise above and fulfill their dreams. Giving these kids a chance to improve their learning skills. They now have access to books, computers and other learning materials. Games, sports and activities that stimulate their minds and open their eyes to a brighter future. I want this for them, I want these children to have a better start in life than I had years ago.

But that's not all I'm thinking about, because while this will bring me joy, there's the concern for my safety and that of my family members. How can I protect them from this, from the intrusion this wealth has brought us? My God, why am I going there? A week ago, this was the least of my worries.

When you grow up poor, you assume the rich people you envy at times have no problems, because their money has chased them all away. You're so wrong about that, just look at me now. For every million dollars, there are ten problems popping up in my head. Now that I have more money than I can spend in a lifetime, all I could think about right now is how not to become a target it.

I'll have to bring this up with Mr. Daly tomorrow night over dinner.

DANIEL DALY

Even at the age of sixty-four, life was still surprising him. He has had to let go of many things over the years, most of them not by choice. Five years ago, he lost his wife Lisa to breast cancer.

Around the same time, he was planning to retire and hand over the law firm he'd built thirty years ago to his daughter Lily and the other senior partner. But Lily had persuaded him to carry on for another five years.

Those five years will be up next month on his sixty-fifth birthday, a normal retirement age for most people.

Daniel has been counting down the days to his retirement and to be able to do something different. What that will be he was not sure. What he was sure about was that he no longer wanted to practice law. It was no longer interesting; all of the excitement was gone. His role in the firm has been reduced. He was now the firm's lead counsel in name only and he only went into the office three days a week, sometimes less. John and Lily are the ones in charge, and he was not complaining.

He felt old and tired, like his mind is no longer what it used to be. But Lily was not buying any of that, she thinks he's just lost interest after mom died. That could be a part of it, but the truth is, he felt like he had given enough time and energy to practicing law. Now he needed something new, something exciting to make him want to get out of bed in the mornings.

The zest for life has left him.

That is partly why he spent most days reminiscing about the way it used to be with a glass of whiskey in hand, sometimes more than one glass as the day gradually slips away, lost in yesterday, daydreaming and wishing he could re-live some of those special moments.

Like graduating law school at twenty-seven; what an accomplishment that was, then meeting Lisa two years later while on a ski vacation in the French Alps. It was love at first sight. They got married a few months later and she became a part of his big plans. One year later they moved from London to Grand Turk, Turks and Caicos Islands where he worked at BARRENS law firm for five years, then in July 1986 he opened his own law firm Daly and Co.

Lisa was the receptionist for seven years until the company began to grow but she began to find it hard to divide her time between work and raising Lily. Lisa was a mom and a wife - her two favorite roles. She used to say, "If you need me just look over your shoulder. I will play the supporting role, I don't want to be a star, you are the star in this family, Daniel."

She supported him in every way and he could never thank her enough for believing in his dreams; for marrying him and following him many miles away from her family and her country to a tiny British Territory she had never heard of until she met him.

When Lisa got sick with breast cancer their whole world came crashing down. He watched her suffer for two years before the disease took her. Losing her was not a part of the script. He never told her of the nights he left the hospital and sat in his car crying for several minutes, unable to cope with the possibility of losing her.

She was no longer standing behind him, and he felt like his star was fading right along with her. But time has healed some of those wounds, bringing with it peace of mind. He has also learned to let go and go on.

He still finds joy in golf and fishing, but his love of whiskey sometimes takes him away from those hobbies, so much so that Lily has become concerned. She makes it her duty to ensure that he come into the firm at least three days a week for consultation work. Like this morning.

There was nothing exciting about this, he had seen and heard it all in the last thirty years. At least that's what he thought until this morning. Daniel had been nursing a bad hangover when he walked into the office to meet with a new client that needed divorce consultation.

He knew that he was not functioning at peak level and would have preferred to hand it over to Lily, but she insisted. Mary, the receptionist said that the client had requested him. He stumbled into his office a few minutes later and there sitting on the couch was the new client. He had forgotten her name and try as he might, he could not recall it.

"Good morning, dear," he said with a handshake. The name never came.

"Nice to meet you, Mr. Daly, I am Destiny Johnson," she said. Oh, did that name ring a bell? There was something about it. He knew at this point that he had messed up, all he could do was apologize and start over.

He offered her a seat much closer to his desk, and as she got up to move, he was stirred by the way she moved her body. She was very feminine, and she looked around forty-five years old, a pretty face, beautiful white teeth and full lips. She had his full attention, but he could still feel himself losing focus staring at her.

He sat back in his chair and reached for a pen and pad, ready to take notes. God, she was looking directly into his face, a face that was not prepared for this moment. He really should have put a little more effort into getting dressed this morning.

For god sakes, most people looking to get a divorce did not show up looking this good, or maybe they don't expect to see their lawyer looking like him. He had drunk way too much the night before and was now paying for it with the mother of all hangovers. Maybe this was more than he could handle, there was something about this woman that was making him think more than he wanted to.

It was time to break the ice. Tapping his desk with the pen, he got down to business, asking her what it was she wanted. He was not prepared for the answer, not by a long shot.

"Mr. Daly, I have just won ten million dollars in the lottery," she said, then fell silent, watching him, not even a glimmer of a smile on her face.

Good God, he thought. Shock and disbelief flooded him, did she just say she won ten million dollars? Could she be insane? Coffee, he needed coffee to clear the cobwebs and make sense of what was really going on here.

He asked for details, and she showed him the winning ticket and the receipt. Yes, she was sane all right, she had indeed won the UK National Lottery for ten million pounds. She had called it dollars, and she wanted an English lawyer to represent her. Who is this woman? Is this really happening?

He placed the call to London to confirm that she was indeed holding a winning ticket, and it was confirmed, the firm officially had a new client and he was going to London within a few weeks.

She was definitely a very intriguing woman, she had captivated him, and it was not just the ticket. Maybe he will find out tonight at dinner, after she signed the contract, of course.

How old was she anyway, hmm…?

CLOSURE

I know that winning the lottery was not just dumb luck, and I really wish I could have conveyed that to my lawyer.

The tears weren't just about winning; it went deeper than that, it was my life flashing in front of my eyes, then coming full circle. It was my life story, the first sixteen years of a sad life, one that bore little to no resemblance to that of the poised woman who sat in the lawyer's office, dearly holding on to her winning ticket.

Everything about my life seemed worlds away from his.

I know that I needed to move forward and accept that I had arrived at a new and more fulfilling destiny; yet that was proving harder than I imagined. For every step forward I made, my mind took me two steps back; it almost felt like learning to swim all over again. The old was drifting into the new, and I saw loved ones who had passed and taken their dreams with them.

Then, I saw the younger me, with her sad face, watching me, wanting to be remembered. Maybe now was the time the time to acknowledge those broken parts, heal them, and find closure. I needed to go back before I can fully move forward.

It was time to go back to where it all began.

I made the drive to Blue Hills, a little settlement in Providenciales where I was born - the only settlement in the Islands with a drive by view of the ocean.

There are times I wish I was not born there, mostly because of what it has become. It has changed so much since my childhood, and not all of the changes are good.

Funny, but forty years ago I thought it was bad, but I was wrong; back then it was vacant, not enough of anything or too little of everything. But it certainly was not this depressing settlement before my eyes right now that looked forgotten by time.

I wanted to paint a new picture in my mind of what it could be today. So, I did…

I saw a board walk the whole length of the beach with sports bars, restaurants and shops selling local dishes and souvenirs. They're all connected, and tourists can walk out of one into the other, all facing the ocean. They can drink and dine, dance and laugh under the sun and the stars to calypso and soca music.

It would be a scene they can tell their grandkids one day – that of a tiny settlement with a breathtaking view of the ocean, where the energy was magical and the beauty unsurpassed.

They can tell them of the times they rented a buggy that took them on a fifteen-minute drive from their five-star hotel in Grace Bay, leaving the acclaimed world's best beach behind to go to the opposite end of the island to Blue Hills.

They did this because they wanted to be on a beach with an island feeling, where there was a mixture of everything. There is where tourists and natives all hang out together, soaking up the sun and the sea and savoring a variety of island dishes, vibes and music.

It's one of the few places on island where a tourist can walk a mere five steps from that beautiful turquoise water and powdery white sand to the sports bars, order an island rum punch with the little umbrella, a slice of pineapple and a cherry on the side. Not that the frills were necessary. With that in hand they can make their way right back to the beach, feet making large powdery prints in the sand as they slowly make their way to the seashore.

It's seventy-nine degrees and barely a cloud in the sky, the gentle sea breeze brush by and in the background reggae music fills the air 'Feeling Hot, Hot' prompting them to shake their hips in abandon to the catchy tune.

They can savour the moment, knee deep in the deliciously warm water as they sip on their rum punch, as sunbathers with their barely clad bottoms shiny with sun tan lotion snooze under the hot Caribbean sun, oblivious to people strolling by and those making laps in the crystal-clear ocean.

It would be a breathtaking scene they would wish could last a lifetime, because Blue Hills would be paradise.

I was two minutes away from my destination when my fantasy ended, and my mind took me back to my youth. I remember when the main street was unpaved and there were about three hundred people living here, no litter and very few dogs, and those that were here had names and owners.

Our homes were smaller, but they were finished, and we were proud to call it home. They were painted once a year and the yards were always kept clean, no abandoned cars on the properties breeding mosquitoes and other parasites, and no old boats on the bay.

I shook myself, I had to remind myself why I was here today. Maybe I should turn on the radio and try to focus, forget about the past or what could be, and make my way to the Methodist cemetery. But to get there I had to make this drive down memory lane.

Maybe it was never good, and I was just too young to understand it, but it was all I had then and there was nothing to compare it to, until now.

Thankfully, I arrived at the cemetery before the memories could overwhelm me. Parking my car on the shoulder of the road, I stepped out and into a big patch of cockleburs, we called them 'prickles' back then.

As painful as it was reaching down to remove about a dozen or so burrs from the leg of my pants and being stuck again by their needles in my fingers, it was a good distraction from where my mind was ten minutes ago. I needed to start over on this beautiful sunny afternoon.

I needed to reel my thoughts into a more positive place, like what brought me here in the first place. The only things in my view now were the beach and the graveyard. I crossed the street, gripping tightly to the bouquet of flowers I was going to put on the tomb that housed both of my parents, daddy at the bottom and mommy on top.

There is a lot that can be said about that, and it put a smile on my face just thinking about it. She would have it no other way, she was always in charge, wearing those invisible pants, so it seemed natural that even in death she would be on top of him.

But they are still together and that was important. Maybe, they were even having a conversation about me right now. I can imagine them saying, "Is that Destiny? The daughter who could not wait to leave home? Always believing that there must be more to life than what she had, and that she was going to find out."

I tried to imagine them seeing me coming and smiling when I sat down next to them, handing over the flowers. The tears welled up in my eyes, ran down my cheeks as I gently sat down on the cold white tomb. I tilted my head back, looking up to the sky, trying to stop the tears from falling. Daddy had been gone for twenty-two years now and mommy for thirteen.

I had some good news to share with them today, but how do I start this conversation? Would they be surprised with what I had to say, or did they see this in me as a child? I really wished they were still here with me, in the flesh, to share in my joy, see the expression on their faces, hear them say, "I am proud of you, child. You did well. You were always the dreamer."

To feel their arms folding me into a hug as we cry tears of joy. If only I could have that right now, there is so much I would like to do for them. I would have loved to take them with me on that plane to London, to have them share in that moment when I collected the check for ten million pounds. Move them out of Blue Hills and away from that yard and that old house where there was no peace to be found. I wished for that.

I've always dreamt of a better life for them, and now I can give that to them, they're gone. I could only imagine what that would have been like for them, if they were here today.

A cool breeze swept across my body and petals from the bouquet of flowers floated away, gayly dancing in the wind. I tried reaching for what was left but more of them floated up and away, brushing against my face and dancing around me.

I pulled back in shock and watched them go, one by one. It was almost like my parents were speaking to me, telling me that they heard every word and they were happy that my dream had finally come through.

Could it really be? I smiled and looked on in amazement at what was happening around me. The petals continued to float and dance in the wind. It really felt like my parents were here in spirit, celebrating with me.

The tears started again, forcing me to cry and laugh at the same time as I watched the petals go higher and higher, twisting and turning as they glided away from me. Then two petals fell back into my hands, and I thought ok, maybe you are going to London with me after all.

I gently pressed them together, put them in my purse and left the cemetery.

I was already in Blue Hills, so I decided to drive to High Rock as we called it back then, five minutes away from the cemetery.

This used to be home for me. I wanted to take a look at the house where I was born and raised, or what was left of it. It was sad in every sense of the word, the old house sitting on the property was old and terribly neglected, no one lives there anymore.

Broken windows and doors barely hanging on by hinges, paint cracked and discolored, baked by years of the sun and salt on wood that was now decayed. Time and the lack of care have changed what used to be. It was no longer our house, just like it was no longer our yard of yesterday.

I wanted to remember the good times of my youth, the memories that were made as a child growing up there but with that decrepit shell of a home standing there, those happy memories evaded me. All I felt was the same toxic energy that almost swallowed me up, the same energy that forced me to make my escape years ago.

Just thinking about it rattled me; I did not leave that yard one day too soon. The people next door and the energy surrounding them were toxic. Every day was a battle to survive the negativity and the vile behavior that came at us in that yard. It was like a curse. Words were spoken harshly and uncensored towards us from adults who seemed mentally unstable. Our future, as they saw it was doomed, and we were going to bring pain and shame to our parents.

I stood there and recalled those times, but I can see now, right there in front of me, how the hands of time had turned on them.

I suppose the Blue Hills of yesterday is long gone.

As I tried to rush out of there, time somehow held me long enough to remind me of some things I did enjoy.

I had arrived in front of what used to be the government yard where our old elementary school used to be. I'm not sure if the school had a name, it was the only one in Blue Hills at the time. This is where we spent our pre-teen years.

The school had about four classrooms, sectioned off with partitions that never made it to the ceiling or the floor, and the doors were never closed. That was a good thing though, because it allowed the sea breeze to filter through the entire building every now and then. This was needed because we had no air conditioning or ceiling fans and you could hear what was being said in every class.

I remember once when my cousin was sent to the principal's office for misbehaving. I'm not sure what he'd done but I know it was not his first time there. You could hear my cousin's bottom being paddled with the principal's leather belt. We all sat there listening to him cry, terrified for him, but with a sense of relief it was not one of us.

But what made me smile about this was the memory of the day after. I could still see it like it was yesterday. My aunt had come racing into the schoolyard, her car swirling loose dust all over. It was like a scene out of a western movie, come to think of it, and we were waiting for the cliffhanger. She opened her car door, slammed it, all the while talking to herself as she stalked into the principal's office to chew off his head for paddling her son.

There were only three cars on the island and no one knew how to drive one before they arrived. So, no one that we knew of had taught my aunt how to drive, just like no one had taught her how to race her car into the schoolyard like Michael Schumacher. But she was a brave woman, and I wanted to be just like her.

I don't remember learning much in that school because I don't think our teachers were the brightest. I don't blame them though, it was just the way it was back then. The school is long gone but some things remained in the government yard, like the well and the water tank. This used to be a meeting place for us kids. The fresh water tank held rainwater and that water was used for drinking only that was under lock and key.

But the well water was used for everything else and it was free. Every morning we would come to the well to get water, dropping our dippers into the well and hauling up enough water to fill up our pails.

Our parents were waiting for us to return but we were in no hurry. We hung out and played a bit until we caught a glimpse of a parent coming our way with a belt in hand. I don't know how we did it, how we were able to balance a five-gallon pale of water on our heads, buckling under the weight as our parents whipped us.

We were beaten for taking too long to come back with the water and we were whipped again when we got home, and they discovered how much of the water was spilled while we were carrying the pails and being whipped.

You would think we would learn from this and not linger the next time, but no, that never occurred to us. At that well we had a moment of freedom to do what we wanted, and we did just that.

We never left the island as kids; our vacations were spent outside of the house. It was either the beach or the well when it was time to cool off from the blistering summer heat. There was a huge trough next to the well and we would pour water in the trough and sit in it, throwing water in each other's faces. Jumping up and running after each other, falling into the grass only to get up and come back and sit in the trough and cool off again.

There were times when the well water was low, and our dippers came up with muddy water that looked like cocoa. Those were hard times. But things got better when they finally installed a pump at the well. Now, we pumped water instead of dipping. We had more water and more time to waste and that's exactly what we did. And we got whipped for that too, but what else did we have to do. Climb coconut trees for coconuts? We did that too. But, it was more fun sneaking into the neighbor's yard and stealing their coconuts. The coconuts they didn't want, until they saw us taking them. Maybe we should have asked them for it instead of taking it, but that would have been too easy, and they would have probably said no because we had coconut trees of our own.

Our other favorite fruit to steal was guinep. We would sneak up their guinep tree with several bags in hand. Sitting high up there so as to be obscured by the leaves, we would swing from branch to branch, whispering to each other as we grabbed handfuls of guinep and stuffed them into our bags.

One time we got a bit too loud, and two dogs appeared out of nowhere at the bottom of the tree, barking excitedly up at us. We went deathly still, our little hearts trying to jack hammer out of our frail chests, scared shitless. The owner came outside and growled at the dogs to be quiet. I'm not sure who we feared more, her or the dogs.

I remember there was a lot of praying that went on, high up in that guinep tree with the dogs prowling around the yard below us, picking up our scent, but unable to get to us and unwilling to let us down. We prayed fervently for an answer and an escape route from God. When we saw the dogs following the owner to the back of the yard we knew our prayers were answered and we made our escape.

I don't think that was our last adventure up that guinep tree though.

I made one final stop in my childhood village.

I stared out towards the lonely and isolated beach with an expanse of seaweed covering the seashore as pelicans swooped down into the water and scooped up their daily meal. The clear blue water was not so clear anymore and the white hole was now a sea of darkness.

Gone were the sound of children talking, laughing and jumping in the white hole with shorts and dresses, never having owned a swimsuit, or even sunscreen to protect their little bodies from the sun's rays. They were unable to swim and clueless to the danger ahead, yet they never missed the joy of endless Summers dipping in the water, running along the shores of the "bay" as they called it in Blue Hills.

I needed more time. I'd just begun to feel a surge of happiness, so I parked the car and turned off the engine. Something about this spot had drawn me in and I wanted to look back.

Ah, this used to be so much fun. I remember my siblings and cousins, all lined up side by side for a race on the jetty. All six of them, ages nine to eleven years old. Who could run the fastest? Who could jump the highest? They started from the beginning and ran the whole length and jumped off into water that was way too deep for them to stand in.

I was the only one in the group who lacked the thrill-seeking, fearless pre-teen stupidity. So, I became the spectator and their scorekeeper. With fear and excitement, I watched them emerge from the water one by one, dark little heads bopping up the steps of the jetty to safety. Everyone wanted to be a winner, so they kept coming up and going back trying to beat the last winner, while I kept hoping they would give up and give my heart a break.

The entire months of July and August were spent at the beach. We learned how to swim in the 'White Hole' where I almost drown. The White Hole was a drenched-out area in the sea, sort of like a kiddies swimming pool in size, four feet deep. How this came about, I don't know, but it became one of the highlights of our summer vacation.

We all learned how to swim there, teaching and leaning on each other. There were no lifeguards or swimming instructors, no beach umbrellas, no lounge chairs, no towels or sunscreen lotions, we just had the beach - miles of powder white sand, turquoise water and clear blue skies.

It was where our spirits soared.

We did not see danger and we were not watched over by our parents. We were free to spend our endless Summers at the beach in Blue Hills. This is what I wanted to remember about my hometown.

As I put my car in drive and begin my last attempt to leave my childhood behind, I found myself smiling. I realized just how far away I am from what it used to be.

Ten minutes later I saw the sign ahead of me - Leeward Highway. It was time to close the door to my past and say hello to my future.

TURTLE BAY RESTAURANT

Daniel stood at the bar in the Turtle Bay restaurant.
He was having his favorite glass of whisky and trying to relax a bit before his dinner date arrived. From his vantage point he had the most beautiful view of one of the best beaches in the world, a beach he knows oh so well, Grace Bay beach.

He recalled thirty years ago when he moved here he was like any of the one million tourist who visited each year, spending his days stretched out on a lounge chair sunbathing for days on end. It was heavenly just waking up to sunny days and then walking on that beautiful white sand that lead to the most magnificent warm turquoise water you've ever seen.

It amazed him that this was going to be his life forever.

No more overcast, gloomy skies and weather that made him feel depressed. But after a month of his new tropical paradise, he had to scale back on his mid - afternoon sun bathing to every other Saturday or Sunday. He had a law firm to manage and a family to feed. Yet he could not give up on the beach all together, that would have been impossible.

He lived a stone's throw away from the beach and in no time, he discovered another reason to be there. Sometimes he woke up at the crack of dawn with too much on his mind and unable to go back to sleep, so he would sit on his balcony waiting for the sun to rise in the east. Soon he wanted to watch the sun come up each day, but closer than his balcony allowed, so he began searching for the perfect spot on the beach.

Between sips of whisky, he recalled how he would make a point to set his bedside clock to alarm at five-thirty, then he would brush his teeth, wash his face and put on his favorite swim trunks, the one that made him look like he was wearing the Union Jack. After putting that on he would slide his feet into his flip-flops and make two cups of tea. The other cup was for Lisa.

Grabbing a lounge chair, towel, sunscreen and the tea mug he would head to the beach. He could never experience this kind of weather in the UK most times of the year. He knew he was in paradise and he made sure he enjoyed every minute of it.

It usually took him only two minutes to walk through the lush palm trees and on to the board-walk serenaded by the thump of his steps and the occasional chirp of a bird or two in the trees above. He would position his chair, spread his towel, and lie back, waiting for the new day to unfold.

Soon after he started this ritual, he saw that he was not the only one who enjoyed the calm and peacefulness of the beach in the wee hours of the morning. Beach lovers strolled along the sand, some dipping their feet in the water along the seashore while others sat facing the ocean, chatting with each other as they all awaited the new day.

To him each dawn was different. Each time he saw the sun rise at the beach, that big round orange glow slowly rising from behind the moon, it evoked feelings in him that were hard to describe. And those feelings were different every time.

Lisa would sometimes join him and spend more time looking at him instead of at the sunrise, trying to make sure he was not losing it. She would say, "I don't understand how you could do this so many times a week, after all it's the same sunrise. What are you looking for? Jesus?"

He would just smile in her direction and bring his focus back to the East where the sun was halfway visible, and the sky overhead was clearing. He wanted to engage her, to explain his fascination, but he knew she was not there because of it, she was here because of him, and that was good enough.

He looked down at what was left of his whisky, it was mostly ice. Using the straw, he stirred it, not sure he wanted the taste of diluted whisky this evening. He pushed the glass away while bringing himself back to the present.

It was almost eight o'clock in the evening and he was slowly losing sight of the beach and thinking about his new client. He felt elated around her. It's like she turned on something in him and gave him a new lease on life.

He was fully in the present when he heard his name being called and zoomed in on his son-in-law Jack Shaw approaching him. He sighed, this was going to call for another whisky, one he hoped to finish before Ms. Johnson arrived.

I saw my lawyer standing at the bar having a drink and talking to a man about half his age. Another lawyer I guess.

The man was looking in my direction and seemed to be checking me out. I, on the other hand, was checking out my lawyer. From a distance, he looked pretty relaxed and cleaned up. He was wearing a navy jacket that was a bit too heavy for the warm weather, khaki pants and a blue shirt with no tie.

He had clearly tried.

By the time we were seated at our table, I realized that Mr. Daly had made even more improvement to his appearance. His eyebrows were less bushy, and his nose hair no longer peaked out inquisitively at me when we speak. Was I supposed to make a comment on his appearance or just ignore it?

I went for the latter. He is only my lawyer, not my date. He did not compliment me, and I was all right with that because how I looked had nothing to do with why we are here. Like he had pointed out yesterday, this was a business dinner.

He proved that when he reached for his briefcase and handed me the contract.

"We will get to that later, for now let's order a drink, shall we," he said, signaling for the waiter.

I was having dessert and still feeling the buzz from my second drink when I realized it was time to let my lawyer know a few things about me.

"Mr. Daly let me put this out there before I sign this contract - I don't have the schooling that you have, that goes without saying. I don't have the diplomas and degrees that you have earned, and my use of the English Language cannot match yours.

"As I'm sure you've already heard, here in my country we leave the letter S off most plural words. The letter V is used in the place of W, and vice versa. The word HAVE and HAS are misplaced, and so are WILL and WOULD.

"But, please don't underestimate what I know just because I don't have your level of education. I am aware that I am holding a lottery ticket that is worth ten million pounds and not ten million dollars. In dollars it would be less. I know the British Pound and the US Dollar are two different currencies. I am also aware that if I invest my money wisely I could live off of the interest."

He was looking at me with a blank stare, almost as if I had just sprouted horns and started speaking a foreign language. Or maybe it was because I had ended my little speech a bit abruptly. Belatedly I wondered if I was rambling, but it felt good to have it all out in the open, so I decided to laugh at myself.

As peals of laughter escaped my lips, that blank stare slowly disappeared from his face.

"Are you finish, Ms. Johnson?"

"No, Mr. Daly, I am British," I replied, sending us both into peals of laughter. Maybe our hilarity had something to do with my two glasses of wine and his three, but right now it felt good to laugh at my silly joke, breaking whatever tension remained between us.

"You're British, not Finish? Where did you come up with that one?" he laughingly asked.

"It's not where, it's why. I saw that look on your face and I wanted to lighten things up a bit. I wanted to make you laugh and it worked."

"It sure did, so let's toast to understanding each other," he said. I had finished my wine, so I toasted with water and he did not object to that. He did not comment on the things I had said earlier either, but I knew he understood where I was coming from.

The way he was looking at me as I rambled on said it all. Now the question is, will he remember any of it tomorrow.

After signing the contract, we talked some more, getting to know each.

I was surprised at how comfortable we were around each other, the way we chatted and laughed, and I soon felt that I'd made a good decision hiring him. We were the last ones to leave the restaurant. He walked me to my car then went back into the lounge to wait for his daughter to pick him up.

On my drive home, I was still thinking about how lovely that dinner meeting was and how I now had a lawyer who was going to look out for my best interests. He wanted me to understand how much my winning ticket has and will change my life, and he went out of his way to explain it to me.

What I remembered most was when he told me he had spent thirty years building his law firm and have seen many clients over the years but none as down to earth as me, with this kind of money.

I wasn't sure how to take that because I was not as comfortable as he thought. No, my feet were not really on the ground, I was still hanging up there, dangling. I was still trying to find my balance, he just hasn't noticed it yet.

When I am around him I lean on him, on his wisdom, and I give myself a break, because when I'm alone with my thoughts I am not so brave. It's all up and down, but I'm hoping at some point to pull it together. I spent all of yesterday walking backward through my life, but I was not about to tell him that.

"This is big, Ms. Johnson," he'd said, "Seriously, do you realize how much your life has changed?" My reply to that was a question, "Has it?" followed by a nervous laugh. I'd felt a little drunk at the time, but I knew where I was and who I was with. I was also very aware of what I was saying, but I'm not sure I exuded the right amount of confidence.

So, I had to say something to him, I had to let him know that I am human and flawed, and nowhere as composed as he thought. Maybe if he were sober, he would have seen it. How could I fake what I was really feeling? I have no idea where this new journey was going to take me, or how it was going to change me, even though I never had to worry about money again.

"Well, my dear," he said, "I am not going to lie to you, and from what you just told me five minutes ago you are not stupid, but this puts you in another league. I believe you have done your research but unless you are an accountant or an investor, there is a lot you need to learn about handling this amount of money.

"We have an accountant at the firm who is more than capable of assisting you with investing your money if you are interested. I also want you to know that nothing will be done without being discussed with you first. I would love to keep you as a client at our firm for as long as possible. This is why I told you that you would be an asset to our firm. I meant that, Ms. Johnson."

He took a breath, then went on, "Now, with that said, I can help you with the legal part but maybe you need a priest or a therapist for the other part."

"Other!" I thought.

I was about to laugh because I thought he was kidding, but he was not finished. "I say this because I have seen people with this kind of unexpected wealth fall into traps of indulgence and not being able to say no to anything money can buy. There is no more 'I wish I could, or I can't afford it', those stop signs are gone and now you have to know when to stop.

"If you think this could be a problem then it's best to have a professional you can talk to and help keep you grounded. Winning is one thing but getting used to handling the fame and attention that it brings is another. This might not have been what you wanted but it comes along with it."

Mr. Daly's drinks were really working for him because he was preaching to me, he was letting me have the truth and nothing but the truth. There was not a glimmer of a smile on his face, just a sermon coming out of his mouth.

He clearly wanted me to be prepared for the other side of the coin.

The smile had left my face too, and I'd gotten serious and focused. He was taking me out of my comfort zone now rather than later. He knew this was all new to me and that I was probably thinking that all I had to do was collect my money and go back to the life I knew. He was telling me that the life I knew was over.

It was time to accept that.

GOLF WITH FRIENDS

Daniel pulled into the golf course parking lot at 9am.
As he put the car in park, he found himself thinking back to the night before, fervently wishing he had not made an ass of himself in front of Destiny.

He got out and popped the trunk of his Nissan Pathfinder reaching for his golf bag. He looked around to see if any of his golf buddies were there and noticed a few of them pulling in behind him.

Their tee time was for nine-thirty on weekends, but they always came earlier to catch up over a cup of coffee or tea. Some of them have not seen each other or spoken on the phone during the week so they had about twenty minutes to shoot the breeze before heading out to the course.

There were six of them playing today, two husband and wife couples, him and Millie. He remembered when it used to be three husbands and three wives, when there was no awkwardness, like today, because they knew each other so well, almost to the point of boredom. The same stories repeated over and over again followed by the same laughter.

There weren't many surprises left because they'd been friends for so long, have heard all the stories and were now finishing each other's sentences. Yeah, even fanning off the endings at times, as if to say yeah, yeah heard that one already. But even that doesn't work sometimes, as they would just keep on talking. A little hearing aid might change that in time, but the dementia, well that's another story.

They are all over sixty, some closer to seventy, but they are all still active, using the time they still have doing the things they enjoy, like playing golf. These were his friends and he came to realize this even more in the last five years after Lisa died. After the funeral, he had no interest in golf or much of anything, feeling like the odd one out, but they rallied around him, making sure he was not left alone too much to wallow in grief.

His game was just as sad as his appearance, but those four tried to make him see otherwise. It was like having a cheering squad for a child learning to walk for the first time. He would hit a ball and while it was still air bound there would be shouts of "you can do it, Daniel", only to see it land in a tree, then it would be "Damn Daniel, you almost got that one."

They refused to let him think his game was as bad as he knew it was. As the years wore on, they eventually set out on a mission to take his mind off his troubles, bringing Millie, a new divorcee into the group.

Hard as he tried, he could not warm up to her or her to him, even though they had both tried in a way, but the attraction just wasn't there. He figured that he was finished with love and marriage and had gotten comfortable with being alone, but that was until two days ago when he met Destiny.

She stirred up feelings he had not felt in years. Something in him came alive. He wanted to lean into her and hold her, feel the warmth of her body next to his. But he had to remind himself that she was a new client, and these feelings towards her could be a problem. Yet, even knowing that he could not stop thinking about her and wanting to see her again. At least, he was feeling something for someone else, even if that person was his new client.

It occurred to him then that he should have asked Destiny to join them for a round of golf today. It would be nice to see her again outside of work and to show her off to his friends, let them see that he was not lonely and in need of being fixed up. She could be his golfing partner instead of Millie. Okay, maybe he was getting just a little ahead of himself now. Destiny was too young for this group and maybe even too young for him; this is exactly what his friends would say if she came around.

When Don and his wife Sarah introduce him to Millie, they made a point of saying that he and Millie were the same age. To them this could be a plus, but today he thought that was a definite minus, it made him feel too old for Destiny.

There is not a single part of his body that does not get excited in her presence. Maybe she feels the same way about him but was too polite to say or show it. Then again, maybe she was done with romance. That used to be him, but not anymore. Things were changing and now he wanted more from life than just this. He wanted to watch the sunrise again with someone he cared about, and he had a damn good idea who that someone was. He felt like his heart was opening up to love again, but he also wondered what love had to offer a sixty-four-year-old man who took more naps than a baby.

Last night he felt like he and Destiny had really connected and was sure Jack had picked up on it when she walked up. He knew Lily had sent Jack to the bar to check up on him, even though he tried to make it seem like a coincidence.

Jack had seen Destiny before he did, and in typical Jack style he blurred out words without thinking. "Well, well look at what's coming our way and looking right at me." Jack's voice trailed off. The woman was not looking at Jack, she was looking straight at him.

"Shit, Dan," he said, as he poked Daniel in his side, "there is a classy little forty-five coming your way." It sounded like he was describing a car. "This must be your date. Looking good, I can see there is still gas in her tank, all you have to do is get in the driver's seat and start her engine. Daniel Daly, I think you are about to get laid and you have my approval. Now I can see why Lily was worried," Jack said grinning approvingly from ear to ear.

"Yeah, I can see the sex appeal and the overall attraction, and I promise you I will not tell Lily about this." Daniel looked over at Jack, barely able to believe what he was hearing. His son-in-law whose surname should be 'Ass' was spying on him. Who would have thought?

By the time he put down his drink and turned around, she was right there, standing next to him, smelling as good as she looked in that fitted red dress that clung seductively to her curves. Silver stilettos added at least four inches to her height and superb definition to her legs. She had the sweetest smile and when she parted those full luscious lips of hers, visions of sinking his into them assailed him.

She must have read his mind, because she leaned in and kissed him on the cheek. "Good evening, Mr. Daly," she said with a smile. Daniel remembered the dinner, signing the contract, and having to reassure her that all of the information she has so far divulged was strictly confidential and for her not to worry about it making the news before they got to London, if ever.

He recalled her little speech where she revealed she knew the difference between the US Dollar and the British Pound, among other things. A worried Lily had picked him up ten minutes later. She had wanted to join them for dinner, but he had insisted that he was more than capable of handling a contract. She had replied that it was not the contract she was worried about, which made him smile in the darkness of the car, thinking that she was right.

MEETING LILY

Hello, I said as I walked into Mr. Daly's office.

I did not realize that there was going to be three of us. My attention was immediately captured by his female lookalike. She was sitting at his desk and looking straight at me, seeming to suck up all the energy in the room, green eyes beaming at me like headlights.

I was not sure whether it was admiration or inspection. My delight at the prospect of seeing my lawyer began to waver, besides, he was nowhere in sight. Maybe I'd stepped into the wrong office? But before I had a chance to ask, she spoke. "Hello, Destiny, come on in."

It seemed so informal to hear someone in this law firm call me Destiny. You would have thought we were friends. I got closer, and extended my hand, "Hi, and you are?" She flashed pearly white teeth that glistened in the sunlight filtering through the windows, stood up and shook my hand with authority.

"I'm sorry, I forgot we haven't met as yet. I am Lily Daly-Shaw. I am a partner in my father's law firm."

It felt like she was sending me some kind of message with that little introduction, but the signal was not so clear. "Nice to meet you, Lily," I said with a smile, then launched right in with, "So, you are the Lily who has been calling me, and making arrangements on my behalf," trying hard not to show my true feelings at this intrusive behavior.

"Yes, that was me," she said. She was still smiling and shaking her head, seemingly very sure of herself and me. My words and confidence slowly started to fade at that point, but I gripped tightly to what little there was left, maybe it was time for her to tell me why she was sitting behind her father's desk and welcoming me. I had not come to see her, and as pretty as she was, I was not getting good vibes from her.

41

I had not quite made it to detesting her, just yet, but I was thinking that she was not going to be one of my favorite people in this law firm. I wondered why I was feeling this way about her, after only having met her a few minutes ago. I am not sure, but this face to face didn't appear to be going well for me.

So far, everything I'd heard about her were good, and they all came from her dad. Mr. Daly was super proud of her, she was another brilliant lawyer just like him. He was retiring in a month and leaving his law firm in her hands. He had told me at dinner that Lily was the female version of him. I guess that's a compliment to her. She sure as hell looked like him, but I liked him more.

I tried to shake off the budding resentment towards her, reminding myself why I was there. Any resentment or jealousy I felt towards her was immaterial to that. But it was hard convincing myself, as I had always longed to be where she was in life – educated, career-driven and accomplished. Maybe not a lawyer, but a therapist or a professor, even a famous author sharing my passion with the world.

I'd longed for the gift of knowledge, a career, but somehow that never happened, and I was just starting to accept that it was not a part of the plan. I did not choose my fate, it chose me. For years I'd felt like my fate was to be small and invisible, standing on the outside looking in, longing for the chance to be something more.

Now is that chance - life had just flipped the switch and given me everything I needed. I knew that it was going to take some self-purging before I get comfortable with my new station in life. Thankfully, Mr. Daly walked into the office at that point, snapping me out of my reverie and his daughter from having to comment on my continued silence.

"Hello ladies," he said, looking at me then at Lily.

I turned and faced him with the biggest smile on my face, I could not have been happier to see him. He had a way of bringing me back to my center. There was a balanced energy around him, like we shared something in common. Only God knows what that is. He nodded his head in my direction but did not offer a handshake as his hands were full. He moved swiftly toward his desk and put the papers down in a very uniformed fashion.

Lily got up from the chair to help her dad before coming around the desk to sit in a chair next to me.

Mr. Daly sat behind his desk and proclaimed, "Let's get to work, I have a lot to do today." He was all ready for business and so was I. We were all sitting around at his desk now, with what I assumed was paperwork all lined up and ready for me to sign. Then he said, "Sorry, I don't think I have introduced you two. Lily meet…"

"You are late, dad, we have already introduced ourselves."

"Yes, we have introduced ourselves, Mr. Daly," I said. "I found out a few minutes ago that Lily is a partner in your firm."

"Good," he said. "Well, I guess she also told you that she is going to London with us next week," he said, then gave his daughter a look that I couldn't quite figure out. It left me wondering if maybe she had lied about that in order to force her dad's hand into agreeing with her so as to prevent a confrontation in front of their new client, because I certainly do not recall her being part of our London plans.

I wanted to ask why she was going and get to the bottom of that look, I really did, but given that I had just moved into this calm space and was happy to see my lawyer, I felt a refusal may come off as unreasonable and maybe a little petty. It would probably lead to me being called a bitch behind my back and I wasn't going to let that happen.

Lily was obviously one step ahead of me, come to think of it, they were both steps ahead of me. I might have the money, but these two had the brains. I had to try and keep up. This was another lesson for me. Two against one, what did they know that I don't. Hmm, let me see, everything. But that is why I'd hired them.

"I have a golf game at five, so let's get to it, do you ladies mind?" he paused, looking at both of us as though he was expecting one of us to object. We both looked at him and shook our heads no, and he carried on.

Handing out sheets of paper he said, "Ms. Johnson, here is a copy of the claim form from the lottery office. Make sure it is filled in before we leave for London. This is a list of the identification that is required, this is very important so double check this one, please. This list is about celebratory stuff like presenting the check, photo ops and media.

"As you know, we are planning on leaving for London on British Airways on the fourteenth returning on the twenty-fourth. The lottery has confirmed an appointment for us at their office on Monday the eighteenth. We were advised that the paperwork might take two days to complete and the money transfer five days, but nothing more. Any questions so far, my dear?" he paused, peering over his glasses at me.

"Yes, when do I get to have some fun?" I asked.

Without missing a beat, he said, "As soon as you get your money. I need you to sign these forms so that I can set up the account to have the funds wired to you. I have already started the paperwork, but I need some ID's from you. Did you bring any of them with you? Like your driving license or passport? We need to make copies."

"I will make the copies, dad," Lily said, taking the cards from me and leaving the office. Finally, Mr. Daly and I were alone.

I thought this was the perfect opportunity to broach the topic of Lily going to London with us, but my lawyer got busy moving around pens and papers on his desk and searching his desk drawers, pulling out sheets of paper and putting them back in. Hmm, maybe he knew I was going to use this opportunity to bring it up and was trying to avoid that particular conversation, so I decided to keep quiet and waited for him to look up. That took a while.

Two minutes later he seemed to remember I was sitting there and said, "Sorry I don't have much time today, Ms. Johnson."

"Please call me Destiny," I said.

"Okay, Destiny, as I was saying I have a golf game with two old friends at five o'clock. I tried to change the time but was unable to do so. When I realized I could not change it, I asked Lily to help me with the paperwork so that it will be completed and submitted this week for the company to be registered."

"If not, there will be a delay in your money being wired to you and I don't think you want that, right?" He looked at me with a smile and I smiled back.

"Not at all," I said.

"Well, good we are on the same page," he said. Not exactly, I thought, but he was not letting me in. Maybe the rush was designed to keep me out of the loop. Or maybe I am being a little paranoid.

Lily interrupted my thoughts with, "Okay, here are your ID's and copies of the company's formation forms for your home file. The registration will be ready before we leave for London next week. "So, we are good to go now," as she breezed back into the office, clapping her hands together in victory.

She was done and very proud of herself, but I had one more question. "Wait, I know we have agreed on travel plans but nothing on hotels or car rental," the words were barely out of my mouth when Mr. Daly said, "If you don't mind, Destiny I left that up to Lily. She lived in London while attending law school where she graduated seven years ago so she knows that city like the back of her hand, so to speak."

"Oh, come on, dad you know London just as well as I do. It's just that I know the hipper side of London." They were all chatty and smiling and I felt left out.

"That's the London she is interested in, I'm sure," he said. Why not ask me I thought, after all I am sitting right here, but no, this was between Daly and Daly.

"Lily," he said, "I have not been to England in five years. I assumed a lot has changed since then and not all good. You on the other hand were there for a friend's wedding in November last year."

These two were making me tired, talking over my head like I wasn't there. They can certainly keep a conversation going, but I could have cared less who was the first person or the last person in London. I knew where I wanted to stay in London.

Watching them, it felt like the invisible me was back.

"Listen guys," I said, "we are pressed for time, so I suggest I email both of you the hotel that I would like to stay at in London."

I'd finally gotten their attention. "This will be my first time in London and I would like to make it a memorable one, with the help of both of you, of course." I am trying to be a team player here.

I turned to Lily and said, "I know that you will be joining us," still hoping she would explain why or just decline.

Smiling slyly, she nodded her head and said yes, "I will be joining you and dad." Again, the victory was all hers.

"Okay," I said. "I will choose a hotel, pick a car service and make a list of good restaurants for us to wine and dine in."

"Sounds good to me," Lily said, and Mr. Daly nodded his head in approval.

"One last thing for you, Mr. Daly," I said. "I would like for you to be my official tour guide in London."

Pointing to his burly chest and smiling, Me, he said?

He liked hearing this, I can tell.

"Well, of course you," I said, making a funny face back at him. I wanted to have a memorable experience of London. I have read stories of that city, followed the royal family religiously since Diana married into it and now Catherine. I wanted to see Buckingham Palace, Tower of London, Kensington Palace, Church Hill War Room, Royal Albert Hall and much more. I could feel the joy and excitement blooming in my chest, and I had Mr. Daly's attention.

He was looking at me with a warm smile when he said, "Is that all, Destiny?"

"Yes, that will be all for now."

I will be honored to be your tour guide and show you around London," he chirped back at me.

"Well, thank you, sir," and I bowed to him.

"Destiny," Mr. Daly said, "I guess you are paying for this tour because it just occurred to me, I cannot afford you."

I was on a roll here and I had a reply ready, but this was no longer a conversation between two. Lily chimed in with a smile, looking at both of us and trying to sum up what was going on in front of her face.

"I agree with dad." Lily had a way of letting you know she was present, unlike me. She was a lawyer and I was now their client. To her, it was all about the money.

So, she was taking over where her dad left off, or more accurately, where she had cut him off. The question was who was paying for all of these extras. This is a business trip, not a holiday. Any meeting with them was on the clock and Lily wanted to make sure I understood that. My happiness was seeping away, leaving me exposed. Lily was waiting for an answer. What is wrong with this picture, I thought. Why do I have to explain myself to her? The conversation was between Mr. Daly and I, not her, and until she chimed in, I think Mr. Daly was making a joke.

I had to find a way to ice her out. Does she always have to be so serious? I am worth millions of pounds, I can more than afford to pay for a tour of London. But maybe it's not the money that's bothering her. It appeared that Lily wanted a clear delineation of the attorney client relationship between her dad and I. She did not want us to become friends. I was certain she was going to find me another tour guide as soon as I walked out that door. But I was feeling good, and I intend for my mood to stay that way.

I said, "No need to worry, I have it covered. Remember, I am worth ten million dollars," and with a big smile on my face I picked up my bag and said goodbye. I could hear her over my shoulders saying, "It's not ten million dollars, it's ten million pounds. For the love of God, get it right Destiny. Dad she is clueless."

FIRST CLASS

.

I was going to stay in a five-star hotel, because I can afford to.
I could finally treat myself to the things I love. I was paying for
this whole trip, so I could choose whatever hotel or restaurant I
wanted. Knowing this, I wondered if I should take my daughter with me.
After all, Mr. Daly was taking his daughter with him, even though I don't
think it was his choice.

Probably to make it seem like they were not taking advantage of me, Lily
had asked me to choose a two-bedroom suite for her and her dad to share.
Really, I thought. Mr. Daly's only request was to make sure there was a desk
in his room for him to work from. At this point, all I really wanted to think
about was finalizing my plans and the pleasure that came from doing so.

My daughter Anna would revel in the excitement of it all, I know. She
would enjoy shopping in Top Shop, Burberry, Zara, H&M and Harrods.
Should I tell her? My feelings are still mixed on this one. This is too big.
Not to mention, this is my moment and it has already become 'Three's
Company'.

I really didn't want to make it four, besides, I could almost see Anna and
Lily clashing. Both wanting to be the center of attention and me wishing
neither one of them was there. I love Anna and all, but no, I will not be
taking her with me. Over the years I have shared a lot with her, stood
behind her and watch her take center stage without me. Now it's my turn.

I am doing this on my own, and without guilt.

When I return from London I will sit down with her and tell her the
good news. Then I will tell her that her university tuition is paid in full. Just
thinking about that brought tears to my eyes. What a load off my shoulder
this is. I knew that moment will be priceless for us.

Why is winning the lottery bringing up so many issues for me? Maybe
this is what Mr. Daly was trying to explain to me at the restaurant - the

things that I could not see before winning, or things that I thought would be so simple are not so simple anymore. Like telling my daughter.

What am I afraid of really? Well let's see. I don't want her to abandon her dreams now that we no longer have to worry about money. I don't want her to think she deserve to be treated better than others now or lose respect for people who don't have the things that we can now afford. I still wanted her to pursue her dreams, aspire to be great at something. She has so many opportunities I wish I had at her age.

She must continue with her education, get that master's degree, find a good job and earn her way. Yes, earn her way. I wanted her to understand the struggle it was for me to get here. Yet I wonder if that was even possible, because she didn't live the life I did growing up. I never had any of what she has at her age. My whole life was a struggle. My glass was always empty, and I told myself it was half full. I kept myself out of hell by calling it my heaven. She doesn't know what that feels like.

Anna is a product of the generation of entitlement. I don't want her to think she will get whatever she wants because we can afford it now. How do I stop this? This is another thing I'm afraid of. I needed to wind down.

I have been doing way too much thinking and processing. My mind has been like a roller coaster since I discovered I had won the lottery. I had to find a way to relax and quiet my mind. I have gone from feeling incredibly lucky to feeling very insecure and unsure of myself, even to questioning my blessing. Not whether I deserve to win it or not, but if it was worth the emotional roller coaster it has put me on.

I have yet to feel really calm and contented. It's like the money had a life of its own, and I was supposed to follow it. But I don't want to follow it, I need it to become a part of my life. It feels like two different worlds right now. What am I supposed to do with my life? Forget about it? I am trying to take charge, to stay on track, but it's not happening. Maybe, I don't need to be in charge, but I want to know where I'm going, and I don't.

Even my lawyers know more than I do. Something tells me that they are not telling me everything. I suppose I can ask them to tell me what I think I don't know. But maybe if I question them they would feel the same way I'm feeling now, like I don't trust them. I really don't want that because I cannot do this on my own.

Then it hit me, anxiety. I have been here before, losing control because my mind was all over the place. Look at me, all suspicious and nervous, losing faith in my lawyers and questioning what has been given me. It's a cruel fate. I have to calm down or I was going to have a nervous breakdown. I cannot afford to lose my mind over this. I can just imagine the fight that would ensue over who has power of attorney over my winnings.

Did I sign that form, just in case? I'm sure I did, and I am sure I did not give my lawyer power of attorney. Oh God, no, let's not go there. I must take a pill to relax, where is it?

The thing is, every time I think I relaxed a bit, my mind goes racing off in another direction and most of the time it goes backwards. It felt like a rollercoaster ride. Things have got to balance out soon. I have this inner chatter that has not caught up with my outer self, but we need to be on the same page or we were all heading for a meltdown.

I now have more money than I need, and it can take away a lot of my worries, but so far it has only stolen my peace of mind. It's pushing my panic button. I feel like I'm on high alert all the time, there is this keen sense of awareness and the need to read more into things than there is.

Sometimes I'm not even sure what I'm reading. I have signed so many documents and forms in the past week – there is a folder full of copies to prove it. I know I need to read them again, but I can't. There is so much lawyer lingo and most of it goes over my head. It only makes sense when my lawyer is explaining it to me. I really hope I did not sign my money away. It's not like I was drunk when I signed those papers, but I don't remember reading the documents, or being told to do so. What I kept focusing on were all those zeroes. I had never seen so many zeroes and all of them belonged to me.

I need to hire a secretary or personal assistant, there is so much to do and so much I need to learn. I can probably start by taking a crash course in money management. But for now, I should be out celebrating my wealth, dancing like there is no tomorrow, pouring champagne and toasting, shouting to the world that I had won. I did do a little bit of that actually – I'd shouted, danced, cried and laugh, then cried some more. It may have been done in the privacy of home, but I'd done it.

I'd even cried in front of my lawyer. I'd gone through those emotions, only to end up here – anxious. I tried to refocus my mind on my winnings, how my dream had come through. Some may call it luck, but I wondered if there was even such a thing. To me it was a gift from the universe. A gift is a blessing, and this blessing is part of my fate. It was part of the universal plan for my life.

For years I played, believing that I was going to win one day. There were moments when I felt I was wasting my money, when finding out that I did not win left me very depressed. Yet I knew that it wasn't losing in that moment that made me depressed, it was a life filled with trials and disappointments.

I felt I was chasing a shadow and I wished to stop but I found it hard to get comfortable with poverty. If I had to quit, then I had to die, because I did not want to live like that. After trying so hard to change my lot in life, how do I accept defeat? No one judged me harder than I judged myself, and I believed that if I had the ability to try, it was possible for me to make a change, or I would die trying. I wanted a better life and I wanted to believe that it was possible.

Come to think of it, my lawyer might be right, maybe it was time I have a talk with a therapist. I reached over and turned off the light on my nightstand and pulled the covers over me. The pill was finally starting to work its calming magic. I said a prayer asking God to calm my nerves. Could you imagine, that's all I could think of to ask God for tonight. That was it. That was all I needed, peace of mind.

I was a bit tempted to ask him what he wanted me to do with the money. Like does he have a plan for how I'm supposed to use it? Because I could not possibly think he wants me to keep it all to myself. Does he? No, I don't think so. Somehow, I believe he trusted that I will know what to do. But I needed help.

I closed my eyes, trying to clear my mind - tomorrow is another day after all.

As I laid there in the dark bedroom and my mind emptied of the day's worries, an image of a younger me, slender arms outstretched and poised to take a leap, flitted briefly before my eyes; I smiled contentedly and drifted away into darkness' welcoming embrace.

I needed reassurance, so I looked around to see who was watching me.

Who would see me and come to my rescue if I needed it, because I was never a good swimmer, but today I wanted to change that. I stood there preparing myself to jump into the 'white hole'.

I longed to be as fearless as the others, no longer a spectator, but brave. So, brave that when I jumped into the 'white hole' I was not going to drown, I was going to swim. So, I counted to three and I jumped in, kicking against the current and flapping my arms in the water, but going nowhere. I moved my hands to my face, wiping away the water and in seconds I felt myself sinking. I had nothing to hold on to and no desire to cry, just a feeling to fight and to swim my way out of there, but I didn't know how.

"Destiny, you can do it," is what the voice said to me.

My feet were dancing beneath me, and I was clawing at the salt water with my hands, doing anything to stop myself from going under. My face was sinking, but I kept pushing up and reaching for air, taking it in and spitting out water at the same time.

I am eight years old, fifty-five pounds and all alone. My body was getting tired and my legs were moving less with each passing second, I could not think of a way to swim out of there as hard as I tried. There was nothing to grab or hold on to, just water and it was bigger than me. It was covering me all over and I knew I had to swim, I had to try, I had to. I pushed up and it pushed back, I was yanked back down into the water so fast that I went completely under, holding my breath. At that moment I realized that I was still alive and sitting on the bottom of the 'white hole', wondering how to get back to the top and not wanting to die there.

Then I heard the voice again, "You can do this, Destiny, you can swim. You can swim out of here. Don't breathe, just swim." I opened my arms wide and reached up, willing my legs to move with me, pushing my body and stroking the water away from me. Telling myself that I will not die here, I will swim. I will make it out of here.

I felt like time stood still and I was sure of nothing. Please don't let me die here, please don't let me die. I was tired and weak when I finally saw clear blue skies. I dragged my body out, far away from the 'white hole' and stood up to walk but staggered and fell. I got up again and this time I kept going until I reached the shore where I dropped to the sand. For two minutes I threw up salt water, eventually collapsing in my own salty vomit, shaking, scared, not sure how I had made it out.

I was crying, and I was confused. Did someone help me? Or did I swim to safety? I wasn't sure. My little heart was beating so fast I was afraid I was going to have a heart attack. My mind raced. I was alone on the beach, alive. Too weak to get up and walk and more afraid now than ever to look at the 'white hole'. The tears were coming down faster and my cries got louder.

"Why God," I silently pleaded, "why can't you help me to swim. Help me. Help me please."

"I just did," the voice said, "I just did."

A slight gasp woke me up. I opened my eyes, throwing the rest of the tangled covers off of my legs.

I was having that nightmare again.

I gave up on sleep for the rest of the night, crawled out of bed and went to make some cocoa in the hopes that it would at least wash away the remnants of the nightmare and calm my nerves a bit.

It's funny how this win, this ten-million-pound lottery ticket had snowballed into what seems like a giant air balloon. My life was way simpler before this. So many things I could have ignored, and no one would fault me. I did not have anything anyone wanted, did I? Even if I did, there was nothing that made me think as much as I do now.

That little piece of paper that held those six numbers was taking over my life. My days were consumed with how to and how not to. I am now taking anxiety medications to calm my nerves because like my lawyer told me, this is big, this is bigger than me.

I could not have imagined what he meant until now. Therapy may well be my next move because right now there is a good chance that I might have to share my winnings with someone. I was getting comfortable saying I'm a single woman, after all I do live alone and have been for a year. My almost ex-husband does not bother me, and I don't bother him, but I am trying to figure out how me winning ten million pounds after our separation was going to change that. The question is, is he entitled to any of it. This is bothering me, it's practically making me sick. It's my lottery ticket. I played the lottery on my own and with my own money. It belongs to me.

Why hadn't I filed for divorce like I said I would when I was angry with him? I knew that seething anger was serving a purpose. A year ago, I was really steaming, some of it was practically coming out of my ears. I could have knocked him into a hole and buried him alive; that was how pissed off I was. I had seen all the wrong in him and could have convinced any judge to give me my freedom, and today I would not have had to seek counsel about this aspect of my winnings, or worse lose sleep over how he would hire two lawyers to my one to take half of my winnings away from me.

Right now, he and I are in a good place, but he does not know of the win and I have lived with him long enough to know that he would not let me keep this money all to myself, even if a judge said it belong to me alone. I also knew with absolute certainty that he would not take less than half. Money is God to him. I think me winning one day and him not being a part of it was one of his fears.

For Pete's sake, I won the lottery miles away from where he lives, in another country to be exact. Tell me how he was going to find out? Who was going to tell him? But something tells me that he will find out, and when he does he will rain down hell fire on me if he realizes that I am trying to keep it from him. It will be worse than giving up half. The only way to find out if he is entitled to half is to ask my lawyer, but right now, I don't want to do that.

Why would I want to mess up a perfect moment with something like that?

Bringing up my husband right now was out of the picture, it will steal all of the beauty and joy of this moment. I'd lived with him for fifteen years and he always had to be the star of the show. It was always about him; but this time it's about me. I will take my chances. I will not tell him because this belongs to me.

Can't I just go to London and collect my money? Stand in the moment with people who are only there to support me instead of hogging the spotlight. Can't I just have this? I know I have to file for divorce and I will, but right now I wanted to focus my attention on where I felt whole, not broken. One day I will explain this to Mr. Daly, but not now.

Maybe it's time I call that therapist he had recommended.

LILY AND JACK

Lily was preparing for her trip to London.

She was wondering what was more difficult – bulldozing her dad into letting her go to London with him and Destiny or telling her husband Jack that she will be away for a week.

She knew she had painted her dad into a corner with her announcement in front of Destiny, making it hard for either one of them to tell her no, and she knew Destiny may have suspected what was happening and probably resented her.

She feels like there is a catfight waiting to happen between them. It's not like she wanted Destiny to become her best friend, but a good business relationship would be nice.

That little uncomfortable situation with the London trip aside, Lily had gotten a sense that Destiny didn't trust her or like her at all. Shit, that is the same feeling she had with girls all through university and law school. What was wrong with them? That's why her closest friends are men.

She shrugged it off, dismissing Destiny's feelings from her thoughts. This was business after all, and she was not going to let any personal issues get in the way, at least not before the ink was dry. She needed this client's money and she was willing to suck it up to get it.

In a month, she will be the boss and under her belt will be the rich new client, all because of her. Now all she had to do was inform Jack that she will be going to London with dad next week. She was not asking permission, she was telling him.

Jack heard Lily all right and he was not buying her excuse for going to London with her dad. She was laying it on too thick, telling him that her dad needed her in London and that this client was very important to their firm.

Jack, with his limited knowledge of what his wife's job entailed, only saw Lily's going to London as being her dad's bodyguard and he said as much.

"Let me guess, is this the client you sent me to spy on? The same one your dad had dinner with a week ago? The one you think your dad wants to shag? You are going to tag along with him and his new client and leave your husband at home alone. I seriously don't see how that's fair."

Lily could not believe what she was hearing. Was Jack drunk? "Dad needs my help, Jack! I am not tagging along. I am a lawyer and I work with my dad in his law firm. I know this might be difficult for you to comprehend, given your line of work, but let me be clear, I am a lawyer, not a spy. When I change careers, I will let you know."

Jack was a bit taken aback at the vehemence in her response. "Lily what do you mean by given my job? Are you insulting my job or my intelligence?"

"You don't want me to answer that, Jack," Lily said, "because right now neither of them is doing you any favors."

"You are so damn British with your snotty attitude," Jack shouted back. This conversation had gone off the rails. "You know what Lily, you should have married a lawyer like yourself instead of a construction worker like me."

Those were her thoughts, exactly. He must have read her mind, but she could not bring herself to actually say it out loud to him. There was so much truth in that statement. This was a painful moment and she saw the end of her marriage if she answered. No, she could not do this now. Not now when she was going to London.

She was not going to hurt a man who had done nothing but love her even though she was no longer sure of her love for him. Five years ago, he was all she needed after losing her mom to cancer. Jack's world was different from hers and in that lie the appeal. The complete opposite of her and she craved every moment of it. Her dad had been shocked when she started dating Jack. He never actually said it, but he didn't have to, the look on his face said it all. She suspected that he'd kept his feelings to himself because he was afraid of losing her too.

This was not the time to say goodbye to their marriage, not today, now was time to say sorry. She knew how to get on Jack's good side, so she went to the kitchen and came back to their bedroom with a cold bottle of Heineken beer in hand. Massaging it between her unbuttoned blouse, against her bare breast, all while looking into Jack's eyes.

He was sitting on their bed and was feeling like he had lost the argument until she walked in. He reached out for the beer, letting his hand linger on the softness of her flesh. He planted soft kisses on both, then he took the drink. He knew what was coming because he has been here before and he loved it. He felt the blood rushing to all the right places. He took another mouthful of beer and watched her remove her blouse, her lace bra, exposing her luscious breasts to him.

Oh, he was ready to play.

She took the beer from his hand and drank some, then seductively poured some over her breasts, moving closer to give him a taste. Lily knew what her husband loved, and she was about to give it to him.

This was her way of saying sorry, no words were needed.

WICKED THOUGHTS

Daniel made it to the golf course with only ten minutes left to tee time.

He was in a bit of a rush getting there, but he knew that after their round of golf he and the guys would sit at the bar in the clubhouse to wind down with a few bottles of beer.

Today, it was just the three of them - him, Don and Ronald - no ladies. This is when all the caution and proper behavior flew out the window. He normally felt like a spare wheel, but not so today. He wondered if it was maybe time to let the guys in on the new direction his life was heading.

He had seen a new horizon and damn, did it look good. This feeling could only improve his golf game, he was sure of that. She will be the fuel his life has needed for some time now, improving not just his outlook but his game. He can already picture his friends' astonishment as he swings his club with restrained power and precision, smoothly and perfectly guiding the ball home.

They would definitely not expect that from him but imagine their greater surprise when he reveals what was fueling his new lease on life. He felt safe talking about her now, as he hadn't failed to notice that she was not wearing a wedding ring and neither had she mentioned a significant other.

He knew that those observations did not mean that she was not somehow involved but he felt a bit apprehensive putting the question to her directly, given that they had only just met, and he could not be one hundred percent sure that she was as attracted to him as he was to her. But he felt the tension, the repressed sexual energy that permeated the room whenever they were together, it is so palpable, that she had to feel it too.

He paused for a moment as he lifted the golf bag out of the car, recalling the intensely vivid dream from the night before. He was strolling through London at night, gently clasping Destiny's hand in his as they toured the neighborhood; she looked so serene and contended as she casually leaned her body into his, moonlight playfully mingling with the glow of happiness to form a halo around her face when she looked up at him and smiled.

He stopped and pulled her closer, deliciously crushing her supple curves against his chest, fighting a deep urge to caress every inch of her, as joy and desire surged through every fiber of his body. Big Ben faded into the distance, obscured by the pulsing energy that flowed from him to her and all around them as they stood locked in embrace, staring into each other's eyes with naked desire.

Her hand slowly caressed his arms, his neck, sensuously cupping the right side of his face; he felt his body jerk in response as he tightened his hold on her tiny waist, pulling her so close not even the brisk evening wind had safe passage.

She gasped, parting those luscious lips of hers as if to beg him to devour her. He leaned in, parting her lips with the warmth of his – bliss. He was in her mouth, their tongues entwined, and he joyfully drank in her desire as she caressed his face. Oh, how he would love to remove her clothes and make love to her right now.

When he woke from his dream he was painfully aroused but happy. Destiny Johnson was hanging around in his head like his favorite song. Yes, he wanted to love her in every sense of the word, a lot more than he was willing to say to Lily or anyone. Maybe there was hope for him after all.

He had not made love to a woman in years, and if it was going to happen, it was going to be with her.

HOTEL RESERVATIONS

I chose the May Fair Hotel in London West Minister Borough.
I'd fallen in love with it at first sight; I felt that if I was really going to do this, I was going to do it big.

I chose three rooms, instead of the two Lily had suggested. You don't share a room with your father when you are thirty-five years old, I firmly told myself.

I had decided to put my feelings about her aside and focus on all the good that has just showed up in my life.

Mr. Daly will be in the studio suite, average 485 square feet; lots of space for the big guy, I don't want him to feel closed in. I wanted him to feel at home. I think Mr. Daly deserves this. His room came with all of the amenities a five star establishment like this has to offer – it was contemporary in style with studio features like Wi-Fi, Samsung smart TV, sofa, tea and coffee maker facilities, in-room-safe, and a mini bar, bathtub and separate walk-in-shower with a double sink, bathrobe and slippers, toiletries, walk-in wardrobe, and a work desk with international phone and plug sockets. Maybe I do like my lawyer a little, a bit more than I should.

I'd thought of getting a less expensive room for Lily but changed my mind. While my own room matched Mr. Daly's, I was not so sure Lily's should.

Now on to choosing a car service – this was simple, I wanted luxury, exceptional service and reliability and for all of those things in one package, the price was not cheap. These are my choices and there will be no changes. I intend to convey this to Mr. Daly and his daughter in my email to them, so they can confirm the reservations through the firm's account, which I will of course be reimbursing.

My mind ran on Lily again, and her possible reaction to the news that her demand to share a room with her dad has been ignored. Maybe this will teach her that I am no pushover, irrespective of what she may have assumed from our first meeting. I am well aware what her real role is on this trip – she will be there to guard her father, but I strongly suspect that he in turn intends to take up some guard duties of his own and it certainly won't be of her. That much I am sure of.

At his age, Mr. Daly surely does not need guarding, he is a very capable man. But maybe Lily thinks he needs protecting from me, why that is, I've yet to figure out. I strongly suspect that she thinks I am a strong contender for her father's affections, which she wants to keep it all to herself. From the moment I met her she has rubbed me the wrong way; her coldness towards me and seeming lack of respect has only inspired similar feelings of animosity in me. Given that she invited herself on this trip, if she pisses me off I will be forced to make her pay her own hotel bill.

She may be a lawyer, but I am not about to let her win.

"Dad, I've confirmed all of the travel reservations - airline, hotel and car service, just like Destiny ordered."

"Thanks, Lily, but I don't think she ordered you, she simply requested," Daniel replied.

Lily shook her head, rolled her eyes and put a copy of the itinerary on her dad's desk. "Here it is, just like she requested. Did you notice that your new client gave me my own room at the hotel? She did not put me in the room with you like I suggested."

"You didn't want to share a room with me, Lily. You were forcing her hand and you know it. Or, maybe she likes you," Daniel said with a short laugh.

"Likes me, ha, I don't think so, but I'm sure she likes you, quite a lot," Lily shot back at him.

He looked up, sighed, "Lily, you have nothing to worry about, you are not being replaced in my life. Destiny likes what I am doing for her."

She smirked, thinking and you like what she is doing to you - providing you with good visual and dreams I'm sure. She has seen the way her dad looks at Destiny, his eyes can't hide his desire for her.

"So, how old is she?"

"Somewhere around your age, I guess," he replied. "About forty-five?"

"Dad! Seriously, Lily said, "I am not forty-five!"

"Oh, no? Well, in a couple of years you will be." Daniel knew he was ruffling his daughter's feathers and loved every second of it.

He had just knocked her down a peg and she was fighting her way back, just like she did as a child and now as a lawyer. He knew that she will find a way to win this round. He waited.

"Well, I had Destiny's ID's, and I know for a fact that she is fifty years old," she came back with, smirking.

Who would have thought that piece of information would put a smile on his face? He was delighted, but he tried to conceal it with surprise, "Are you sure, Lily?"

"I am, and you are right to be surprised. I was sure she was around forty-six as well, until I saw her ID."

Well, how about that he thought, maybe there is a chance for me after all. She is fifty years old and don't look a day over forty-five. Oh, he was definitely feeling good. He felt the adrenaline rushing throughout his body just at the mention of her name, right down to that region. Luckily, he was sitting behind his desk and didn't have to get up anytime soon.

He felt young and invigorated, and nothing could spoil that mood, not even his obviously displeased daughter, standing there and doing a poor job of concealing her displeasure.

LONDON BOUND

Lily sat next to her dad in first class.

I sat across the aisle at a window seat. We were finally London bound.

I didn't think it was possible for me to sleep on a plane, it's never happened, but those first-class seats are pretty comfortable. It felt like the next best thing to being in my own bed.

I took a pill to calm my nerves right after they served us dinner and out I went. I must have slept for five straight hours, before nature's call woke me, then back to sleep I went, curled up in my seat like a contended kitten for another two hours.

Hours later I woke up refreshed, my mind clear. I looked over the stranger sitting beside me to Mr. Daly and Lily; both seemed engrossed in conversation with each other. This was the first time I had been in such close proximity to my two lawyers without having a conversation with then.

I really wished I had not snored – those dimmed lights and the comfy seat as the plane glided smoothly across the Atlantic Ocean had really done me in. I wanted to get as much rest as possible for what lay ahead, particularly given the five-hour time difference.

I'd come prepared to step off the plane and into London Heathrow airport looking as fresh and well put together as possible. Lily was not the only one looking camera ready. I wanted to exude a little power of my own before my big moment, so I put a little red in the mix. I was wearing a pair of blue jeans that hugged my curves in all the right places, a stylish short sleeved red jacket that stopped just above the hips, set off with elegant brown pumps. But while I looked practically edible, if I do so myself, the close fitted clothing took a toll on me after being immobile for several hours. I'd traded the shoes in for a pair of comfy white cotton socks.

The last two hours before landing, the reality of the moment began to tug at me with a mixture of excitement and anxiety. I wish I had someone holding my hands right now saying you can do this, Destiny. To lessen the anxiety, I closed my eyes and thought of what Mr. Daly had said to me when we arrived at the airport in Turks and Caicos.

He leaned into me and said so loudly into my ear, it seemed he believed I'd gone deaf overnight, "Do you have the lottery ticket, my dear?"

I giggled, and he looked concerned, so I put my mouth to his ear and whispered, "Yes, I do have it and it's in a very safe place." His expression went from concerned to surprised when I added, "And if you want to find it you will have to strip search me."

"Oh," he said with a wink and a chuckle. "Really, Destiny? Do you want me to strip search you?" He was really enjoying our little flirtation, and it made me smile to see this lighter side of him.

Soon we were both hollering with laughter after I replied, "Only if you want to be dis-barred."

Now here we are ten hours later, about to land in London. I looked over again and saw father and daughter still locked in deep conversation. I was too far away to make out what they were talking about, but it looked cordial. The love between those two was obvious and so was the lineage, there could be no doubt they were related. My eyes lingered a bit longer and I knew I had made the right decision when my lawyer finally looked over at me.

Lily had just gotten up, so now I had a clear view of him. If I only knew what he was thinking. His body was angled in my direction, right hand under his chin, a slight smile on his lips, those beautiful eyes of his seeming to pierce right into my soul from all the way across the aisle, searching. I waited for him to say hello, but words never came, just a warm message communicated through his gaze, 'I got you Destiny. I am here for you'.

I did not know what to say, so I smiled and let the moment speak for itself. Something was happening, I felt like he was sitting right next to me and he was about to touch my face, but the moment was abruptly interrupted when Lily plopped down into her seat, cutting off my view. She looked over at me and matter-of-factly said, "We are in London."

"Yes, we are," I said, and I looked away and out of the window.

We were twenty minutes away from landing.

Leaving the automated passport gate, Mr. Daly inched closer to me, "We are here."

I was about to respond when I saw Lily rushing past us saying, "Come on guys, our driver is out front waiting for us."

"That's what he is getting paid for," I said.

"She is right," Mr. Daly said. "What do you think, that he is going to leave us? Why are you in such a hurry, Lily, do you have a date?"

I felt like I was sprinting with the large half empty suitcase banging against my heel with my every step. Lily was way ahead, but Mr. Daly stayed by my side, like he was protecting that lottery ticket, and me.

We finally made it outside. It was an overcast morning, no sun and a bit of chill to the air. Mr. Daly offered me his jacket to keep warm.

Our driver was wearing a grey uniform, trimmed with black, and a matching hat on his six feet frame. On his name tag was Michael.

He appeared to be about thirty-five years old and quite handsome. I could feel my body temperature rising. Seemed like Lily had gotten the memo, hmm, we may even become friends if she keeps doing her job this well. Michael was a young Daniel Day Lewis lookalike, and I was in heaven. I may have even drooled a little, which I'm sure my lawyer saw, if that slightly irritated look on his face was anything to judge by.

Michael opened the passenger door behind the driver's seat and I slid in, Lily opened her own door and sat next to me. Mr. Daly sat up front with Michael

"Take us to the May Fair Hotel," Lily said, leaving me to wonder who had died and made her the boss. Any goodwill I was beginning to feel toward her evaporated. Here we go again. Seems like I cannot shine for long around her without a fight. Aw well, I dismissed her and focused my attention ahead where a delicious piece of eye candy was sitting just inches in front of me.

I'd tuned Lily out, but I overheard Michael saying to my lawyer that he was told we are here for a lawyer's conference.

"Yes," Lily popped in with, and this time I could not be mad at her. A lawyer's conference sounded like the perfect cover, I love it. I am pretty sure she was the one who had come up with that cover. She really is a good liar… lawyer, I mean. But, is there really a difference? I think they are trained to bend the truth or at the very least leave you doubting what the truth is. Much like I'm feeling right now.

I wanted to lean over to her and say thanks, but the word stuck in my throat.

Instead, I reclined into my seat, blocking them all out, as I brought my body temperature back under control. There was still hope that Lily would engage me in a conversation, but while I waited l looked out the window and enjoyed the scenery. Lily on the other hand began texting on her phone, making numerous calls and catching up with friends. Mr. Daly glanced back at us a few times, probably to make sure his headstrong daughter had not tossed his favorite client out of the window.

As the car continued on its way to our destination, I slowly became of Lily's conversation – she was making her own plans. She was taking the three free days we have before our appointment at the lottery office to visit with friends from Law School.

I am only finding this out now, in the car, on our way to the May Fair Hotel, after I've already booked a room for her. She really does have her own agenda, doesn't she? Maybe this could be the perfect time to get into a catfight with her, hmm, and this time I had a good reason. But maybe her being gone for three solid days might not be such a bad idea, I mused, trying to think strategically. Not only will I be free of her energy sucking presence, I will have time to shore up my confidence without her annoying me before my big moment. This could be good.

I sighed, she really could be exhausting to be around, with her spoiled rotten persona. Clearly her dad had skipped over quite a few pertinent lessons in humility with her.

Trying to seem as unobtrusive as possible, I really observed her for the first time – at five feet eight inches she is quite tall for a woman, pretty, with lustrous dark hair that framed an oval face dominated by those sharp, intelligent green eyes of hers, tiny nose and a cute little bow shaped mouth. She could demand anyone's attention, especially the opposite sex. There was an intimidating aura that always seem to surround her, and I felt it now, sitting in the car just a few inches away from her slim, navy suited figure. She looked lawyerly, yet there was a slight ladylike softness that came through the woman of business image she was projecting to the world. Maybe it was the soft blue polka dot silk blouse that playfully peeked through her classic jacket, and the pink peony smell of her perfume. She wore minimal make up and her fingernails were free of polish.

Her attire screamed power player, and I was sure that was the image she wanted to convey. I sighed, refocusing my attention to the view from my window – there was definitely never going to be any conversation with me about the latest fashion with her, no way. We had nothing in common. I know I was out of her league, but it's not like we were competing for anything. My ten-million-pound lottery ticket will never measure up to what she has accomplished so far in her life and career.

What she does, I could not do it. I could not twist the truth for a living, and neither do I have what it takes to know how to even do that on a professional level. The wall between us – built in part by our differing circumstances and by her barely concealed animosity towards me – was vast, but I still wondered what it would take to tear it down. I also knew that she would never try to meet me at my level, or any level for that matter.

I was reading the hotel's brochure for the third time.

We were almost there, and I was fascinated by the history of it and the nearby attractions. I wanted to know as much as possible about the city of London and about the West End where our hotel was located. This was part of my tour guide's job, but I could not wait until then when I was holding a brochure in my hand.

I dove right in and began reading.

The May Fair Hotel, opened by King George V in 1927, is a luxurious five-star hotel situated on Stratton Street in the stylish heart of London surrounded by parks, theaters, and the attractions of London's West End. The luxury hotel has free WIFI in all areas, a private theatre and a 24-hour business center. Their award-winning chefs source the finest produce to create exquisite dishes. From the May fair Hotel, there is direct access to Canary Wharf via the London underground at Green Park and Knightsbridge can be reached by foot in approximately 20 minutes, and Oxford Street in just over 10 minutes.

Nearby is Westminster, home of some of London's best-known landmarks and seat of government. There was the house of parliament and Trafalgar Square, Big Ben, Whitehall Palace, the Prime Minister's official home and even Buckingham Palace, all within easy reach of my hotel.

I am looking forward to seeing all of these places now that I'm in London.

COVERT PLANS

First, I have to take care of business.

I'd made an appointment at Barclays Bank for 3pm today. This is information I have not shared with my lawyers.

I may not be a savvy lawyer, but I knew enough not to put all of my eggs into one basket; I needed a plan B, if only for my own piece of mind. While there, I am going to open two accounts and have my lottery winnings transferred into them.

After all, I am a British citizen and there is no reason for me to rush back to the Islands, or to take my money out of London. Technically, I am home, even if this is my first visit. I can stay as long as I want. Maybe this is the opportunity I have always longed for, to travel around Europe with Anna tagging along before university starts in September. I may even make it an extended tour, six months or longer. After I've seen and experienced my fill, I can still have the best of both worlds - life in a tropical paradise for the colder months in the year, followed by a more sophisticated European lifestyle for the other half.

I'm an Island girl by heart, I would pick clear blue skies and sun-drenched beaches in the winter, over bitterly cold and mud splattered streets, hands down. I know there is much to be enjoyed and savored here, and I was determined to discover them, with or without my lawyer. My options were truly endless.

As with my plan B with the bank, I have already been online looking for a two-bedroom flat, possibly in Devon where I can see the ocean and still have a feel of the Islands. I could learn a new language, so my travels will be even more enhanced. Take some cooking classes, or even a few dance lessons.

I laughed softly to myself, where is this excitement coming from? Well, while I'm at it, how about fully submerging myself in British history and culture, find myself a lovely gentleman to escort me to the theatre, museums and to stroll hand in hand around the city. What a lovely idea!

It felt good to now see the possibilities that my new wealth has opened up for me. I felt a rush of confidence as London flew by my window; I can do this. I think I'll be staying in London for a while. Change of plans.

Daniel was not taking any chances.

He was not going to let this moment slip away from him, as he was prepared to impress Destiny in more ways than one.

Soon as he had arrived in his suite at the May Fair Hotel he had made some very important phone calls. It was time for him to up his game, he wanted Destiny to see him in ways she never imagined.

He was having dinner with her at eight in the hotel restaurant, just the two of them. How refreshing! Lily had made a quick exit right after checking in, she had other plans. This was making everything a whole lot easier for him. With Lily around there were always questions that he was not prepared to answer; she wanted to know everything he was feeling or thinking. He did not need a shrink, what he needed was love and affection, the kind of love you got from a woman you were not related to.

He had big plans, and he was not going to leave those important plans in the hands of amateurs, so he had hired a personal shopper. She had already been to his suite where she had neatly put away enough clothes to last him the duration of his stay. Each outfit was appropriately labelled with the events for which they are suited. He was determined to get this right.

The sales lady at the Cartier store counter on Oxford Street had helped him find just the right bracelet, one with two entwined hands. To him it said everything, it brought back memories of the first time he held her hands. That moment is now etched into his memory - he remembers wanting to embrace her, offer her comfort and hold on to her forever.

He wondered if at his age he was maybe being a little foolish, but he could not shake the feeling that had come over him, foolish or not. He wanted to do things he used to do thirty years ago to impress a girl. He glanced over at the bouquet of flowers and the bottles of champagne that had been delivered to his room. He wondered how he was going to give all of this to her without her thinking he had lost his mind. Maybe he had really lost his mind.

He grabbed pen and paper, time to devise a foolproof plan. One thing he knew for sure was that by the time he left London he would know how Destiny felt about him. He is a lawyer after all, he will find a way.

After my appointment at the bank I went shopping.

I needed an outfit for dinner later. Mr. Daly had made dinner reservations for the two of us and I wanted to look my best. I also now felt confident that things were coming together for me, after my meeting at the bank.

As we were checking into the hotel, Lily had informed her dad that she was meeting up with friends for the next three days and will not be around. She had then turned to me with a nonchalant, "So, he is all yours."

He managed a distracted, "Okay dear," as I stood there shocked that she had even addressed me. I was barely able to gather my wits to blurt out, "He will be in good hands."

What the hell does that mean? I was so unprepared. I'd felt Mr. Daly looking at me, but I kept my eyes on Lily. Somehow it felt like a beginning for us. Finally, it was okay for me to be left alone with her dad, my lawyer. She had not smiled at me, shook my hand, or even hugged me, yet, but there was hope.

As we took the elevator to our individual suites, Lily continued speaking with her dad about her plans for the next three days and what she was going to do when she returned. Most of it was about me but she was not speaking directly to me. It was a major distraction, and she had to know it, but I did not have the guts to say it to her. Somewhere deep down inside, I wanted her to like me, just like her dad did. But, I knew it was going to take some work.

But distance between us over the next three days was good, I needed my grove back, and I had just the perfect outfit to help me with that.

The suit screamed confidence, and money – it was a deep silk, cream pantsuit; sophisticated and a bit sexy, with a deeply plunging neckline. I accessorized it with a pair of sexy beige high heels, pink pearl necklace with matching earrings, and a cream-colored evening clutch. I was ready for tonight.

I walked out of Harrods looking for a taxi same as I had after my appointment at the bank hours earlier. My driver Michael was busy chauffeuring Lily to God knows where. I was fine with that because I didn't want anyone knowing my every move. There were things I wanted to do on my own and not leave trails for others to follow. Maybe Lily and I had something in common after all; we were both keeping secrets from Mr. Daly.

I arrived back at the May Fair, hoping Mr. Daly had been okay on his own. I thought about calling his suite to check on him, but how would that look. Would he think he didn't need checking up on? Or worse, think I was calling for other reasons, whatever those were. I think I'll just wait until we meet for dinner in a few hours. Those thoughts were put to rest when I entered my room and saw I had a voice message from him. My lawyer sounded very happy about our dinner date and I was just as excited as he was.

I undressed and stepped into the shower, it was time to prepare myself for the beautiful evening that was about to unfold.

DINNER 4 TWO

M r. Daly was already seated at the table, waiting for me.
He was looking like a younger version of Harrison Ford, all debonair and at ease in his skin.

This was not the old Mr. Daly I'd met at his law firm back in Providenciales, no, this was definitely a new and improved version. Damn! I almost lost my step there, I couldn't take my eyes off of him.

Maybe this was part of his plan to capture my undivided attention, and if it were, it was working so well that I'd almost fallen flat on my derrière in a roomful of diners. But I took comfort in knowing that he was equally captivated.

From the moment I entered the dining room, his eyes found and locked onto me, admiration stark on his face. Maybe it was the outfit which I had so painstakingly selected, or, it was that familiar chemistry that always filled the air when we're together. I'll take either one.

He stood up as I continued across the dining room, subtly swaying my hips, taking my time as I advanced on him. The faint scent of his aftershave stirred my senses – intensely vibrant, seductive, with a surprising wisp of freshness to it. I tried to remind myself that no matter how this felt, he was still my lawyer, but the way he was looking right now, I had difficulty forming complete thoughts.

With his hands on my back he leaned in to me, kissing both cheeks and whispered in my ear, "You look ravishing, dear."

"So, you are hungry," I quipped, trying to relieve some of the intensity in the air.

"I am," he quietly growled back.

I managed a little laugh, enjoying the light humor and flirtation between us, but still a little apprehensive to dive in fully. I was falling into something new and being led by someone who was much more experienced than I was. We both had so much to lose. A part of me knew that this was not the way to go, not tonight, but another part of me wanted the thrill of the moment. I could not deny the chemistry between us.

I truly enjoyed Mr. Daly's company, he was such an interesting and intelligent man. I liked the fact that he doesn't feel it necessary to impress me with his depth of knowledge. He may be a big guy in stature, but his ego is well contained, something I find refreshing considering he is a Leo.

He is a cross between a lawyer and a professor when it comes to smarts, and with his wild eyebrows and nose hair that had not been clipped in months, the latter profession would have suited him just fine. But tonight, that disheveled professorial look was nowhere in sight. Could I have had something to do with this new look? I sure hope so, because I liked the improved Mr. Daly sitting across from me.

He must have been quite the catch in his younger, single days; broken a few hearts, I'm sure. I have no proof of this because the only woman he has ever talked about was his deceased wife Lisa. I wonder what his pick-up line was back then to have swept her off her feet so fast. Obviously, he has something potent hidden under that easy manner of his. Yeah, he definitely had something there.

I felt a slight twinge of envy but quashed it before it could bloom. What is wrong with me? What am I doing? Stop it…that was then, and this is now. I am the one sitting at the dinner table with him. Those were my eyes he was trying to lose himself inside of. The bouquet of flowers he had slowly slid across the table towards me had my name on the card, so why am I trying to torture myself with his past. What am I worried about? Maybe I am the one who needs to move on. Or maybe it was time for me to tell him about my unfinished business.

I willed myself to forget everything else and enjoy this magical evening, with my very own Harrison Ford, in this beautiful, luxurious hotel in the heart of London. I flashed him my best smile and watched as his nostrils flared and his lips parted.

Time to have some fun.

Dinner was superb.

As I unlocked the door to my suite I glanced down at the roses, twelve perfect red beauties arranged stylishly in a beautiful red vase.

The card simply read 'Destiny, thanks for being here, Daniel xx.' I walked into the suite, kicking off my heels and placing the roses on the desk. Mr. Daly was thanking me for being with him, while I was still having problems defining the here. Was it just about the dinner, or here in London?

A knock interrupted my thoughts.

I slowly walked over to the door, wondering who it could be. When I opened it, I got the answer to the here: London it was, because my evening was not over. Mr. Daly confidently strolled in, clutching two bottles of champagne and two crystal flutes in each hand, a wicked smile on his face.

"I think it's time to celebrate your victory in style, don't you think?" He opened one of the bottles, poured two glasses. "Here's to tonight!"

We drank to that.

"We need a little music," he said, making himself at home in my suite. "Where is your radio? Let's find a music channel on the TV."

He got right to it, figuring out which of the many remotes on the desk was for the television. I chatted as he scrolled through the stations to find the music he thought best suited the night - Sade's 'The Sweetest Taboo'.

"Let's dance," he said, removing his jacket as he gently swung his hips to the lyrics, moving in on me. I got up in full groove, swinging right along with him.

"Another toast, darling?" he raised an eyebrow questioningly at me, and before I could answer, "Here is to the woman who makes me very happy."

I playfully looked behind me, "Where is she?"

We were both smiling widely, when he moved in for a hug, holding on to me tightly, whispering in my ear, "She is right here."

Oh, how I loved the sound of that. I giggled, and we danced. Mr. Daly clearly had some very specific plans for me, plans I knew nothing of. "My dear, we are going to live tonight without a care in the world."

"Thank God Lily is not here," I replied.

We were on to the second bottle of champagne when he proposed a third toast; I think it was the third toast, because at this point I was beyond tipsy.

He raised his glass to mine, "Here's to a dream I don't want to wake up from."

I chimed in with, "Here's to ten million pounds, just checking," and giggled.

He responded with, "Here's to a new chapter."

"And to me being a big part of it," I finished, swaying in his arms. He kissed me, the moistness of his mouth enveloping mine as his lips explored every inch of my plump lips, his tongue darting in and around mine, stoking our passion.

In the midst of being swept away my mind drifted for a second. Probably sensing this, he kissed me harder, bringing me back to the here and now as he unbuttoned his shirt, revealing his burly chest to me before turning his attention to my blouse. As he skillfully caressed my body, arousing me with his hands and mouth, I leaned back against the wall, thrusting my hips seductively forward and into him to feel the heat of his passion. He was ready, and there was no turning back. The rest of our clothing seem to magically disappear, leaving us naked and wild for each other.

"Oh darling," he said looking at me in admiration, "your body is so beautiful."

Then, looking into my eyes, he lovingly asked, "Should I continue?" I bit down on my lips, nodding my head, drunk with pleasure.

His eyes devouring me, he breathed, "I have dreamt of this moment."

THE DAY AFTER

I slowly stirred awake, stretching and purring like a satisfied kitten. I was not alone in bed. We had slept the morning away, it was now 12:30pm the clock at the side of my bed revealed.

My life had just taken a strange turn, thanks to my lawyer. A turn that had nothing to do with us being here in London to collect my lottery winnings. Or did it? Right now, I don't know, that was the answer to that question, I simply don't know.

At ten o'clock this morning I was planning to visit Oxford Street to do a little shopping, but it was now more than two hours later, and here I am, still in bed. Top Shop, Zara and H&M are going to have to wait.

My plans have changed, and I was having a problem figuring out how I was going to deal with this new direction. Seriously, what do I even say when he opens his eyes? What would be his first words to me? How do we explain this? My God, have I lost my mind? We have seriously crossed the line here. Maybe we should apologize to each other and forget about it, flirting is one thing but, this, this was… I couldn't find the words.

I glanced out the window, worry written all over my face, knowing that I needed to reel in whatever this was, before it became a problem. I sighed at the weather, it was going to be another overcast day in London. What I won't do for a few hours of sunshine, pay cash even, if that were possible. Maybe seeing the sun again might knock me back to my senses. There was little wonder I'd slept through the morning, but then again, we had not fallen asleep until the wee hours of the morning, we were so busy.

I glanced over to my right, Mr. Daly was still fast asleep, sprawled on his back, an arm flung over his handsome face, and a slight smile on his lips. A shower and a pot of coffee is what I needed right now, then when Mr. Daly wakes, we will have to figure out how to spin this before Lily gets back to the hotel on Sunday. For the love of god, we cannot let her know that this happened. That woman would sue me, for what I'm not sure. I'd assured her when she left that her dad was in good hands. I am sure this is not what she had in mind, and until last night, neither did I.

I knew there really shouldn't be an issue here because we're both consenting adults, and I don't have to define or explain my actions to anyone. If anything, the fact that we could still go at it like teenagers, rabbits even, at our mature age should be celebrated. I laughed at the memory, and a little of the anxiety left me, bringing in its wake a slight arousal at the thought of last night. Hmm, maybe a repeat performance was in order, after taking a shower first.

I sat up in bed, looking around the room lit by the light filtering through the drapes, and spotted a box and a card on the desk, next to my roses. How did that get there? I threw off the covers and tiptoed over to it. Mr. Daly had bought me a present and a card, 'To Destiny, thanks for a dream come true. Love, Daniel'. The box was wrapped in gold paper, with a Cartier ribbon around it.

I held the present and card close to my chest and thought of how right this all feels now that I've allowed myself to enjoy the moment. This magical ride has now been enhanced that much more, now that Mr. Daly was going to be a part of it. I kissed the card and felt the love that came with those words. I took them over to the bed, gazing down at Mr. Daly sleeping there so angelically. I softly kissed him on the cheek. I needed him awake so I can thank him properly.

I removed the cover from his body and surveyed it from head to toes, he was in pretty good shape for a man his age, well-endowed too, my god was he ever. I caressed his face, following up each caress with a kiss, until my hands and mouth went on their separate journeys. I felt him coming awake, responding to the touch of my fingers as it flitted lightly down and back up his length, his body jerking as I closed my hand around his thickness. He expanded, forcing my fingers to let go. His body began to move, eyes still closed.

I caressed his face, kissing his neck, and whispered in his ear, "Are you ready for round two? Or do you need a cup of coffee first?"

He was smiled, groaned, and I felt it moving through his chest, down to his nether region. He reached over for me and pulled me on top of him, held me close as he nuzzled his face in my neck. His hand was massaging my back - up and down it went, pausing on my buttocks to give it a squeeze, leaving sparks of desire in its wake.

"Thank you for the gift," I managed to whisper on a breathy sigh.

"Which one?" he asked.

"You don't know?"

"No," he said, "would you care to remind me?" kissing me deeply, his mouth warm and hungry, as his hands continued to stoke fires I thought we had doused last night. My body swelled with delight. He rolled me onto the bed, positioning himself between my thighs, never pausing his sensual exploration, this time to the most sensitive regions of my body, circling and kissing every inch, as his engorged length pulsed urgently between my thighs, sending me wild with desire.

Soon we couldn't take anymore; our bodies joined in the truest sense of the word, just as they did last night.

This time, we were both sober. No regrets.

It was 3pm when Mr. Daly left my hotel suite.

Before he left, we both took a shower, ordered room service and had a light lunch.

There was no I'm sorry about last night, or this morning. We didn't promise not to do this again. Or worst, the dreaded question, what are we doing here? I think we both knew what we were doing. No, we never defined it. We just stayed in the moment.

"I am taking you to the theatre tonight, darling," he said. "We are going to watch the musical MAMMA MIA! You can wear the Cartier bracelet that I bought you."

"Sure," I said, "and thanks again, it's beautiful, I love it," I smiled. I'd finally gotten around to opening the gold box.

"You are beautiful, darling," as he held my face and kissed me on the lips, "you are my dream."

As he was leaving, he gave me that loving gaze again, and said, "See you in the lobby tonight at 7pm, sharp."

I closed the door, and leaned back against it, trying to gather my thoughts so I can plan for what remained of the afternoon. First, I needed a new outfit for this evening. If I had known I would be going out again tonight, I would have gotten two outfits yesterday. I could use a little more sleep before tonight, but who has time.

Mr. Daly is full of surprises, he had even brought a change of clothes when he came to my suite last night. How did I miss that? It was beginning to seem like he had taken over my whole life, leaving me with no time to process anything but him, tossing all of my plans straight out the window. Who would have thought this was possible? Not Me! But I was enjoying it, and it appears that he was too.

Okay, Destiny, I scolded myself, focus now. Ring your driver and tell him you need him to be at the hotel in an hour, you're going to Oxford Street. Time to go shopping. You're not taking a taxi today. Michael should be through taking Lily around. It's time for him to be at your service for a change. After all, you are the one paying him not her, and if it weren't for you, she wouldn't be here in London right now.

AT 4:30pm, I walked into ZARA, ready for my retail therapy.

"Hi dad, how was your night, anything special?"

What a loaded question, Daniel thought, shifting the phone against his ear and shoulder as he stretched.

"Were you on your best behavior?" she added, not giving him a chance to respond. "Didn't drink too much I hope?"

Daniel smiled then, sure that was what she wanted to know from the beginning. He gathered his thought, knowing that he would have to contain his joy and not give the slightest hint of last night, or this afternoon, away to his daughter.

He stifled another yawn as she kept rattling on, damn, it was five o'clock already. He'd only gotten an hour's nap in before the insistent thrilling of the phone woke him. He was sleepy, and happy, but he needed to get some more rest in before he saw Destiny again tonight.

"Lily, my dear," he said when she finally paused for breath, "I am fine. There is nothing special to report here. I was on my best behavior; you can call Destiny and ask her, if you wish." This part he knew was never going to happen, that's why he'd said it.

"And, I did not drink any whisky last night either." He knew this is what she wanted to hear, and it was the truth; the only bit in this little inquisition that was true so far.

Everything about last night was special; he did not need whisky. You don't celebrate with whisky, you celebrate with champagne, and what he really wanted, he'd gotten it. He'd done things he hadn't done in years – wined and dined a woman, made passionate love, and genuinely smiled.

Right now, he was living the dream he's had since the first time he saw Destiny in his office, and he knew he had to keep it between just the two of them for now.

The raw chemistry between them was there from then, and when she'd asked him to be her guide in London, he felt that she was telling him she felt it too.

He told himself that, he was going to take her on a tour all right, and that's exactly what he has been doing. And so far, he has not heard one word of complain from her.

He has not felt this alive in years; he cautioned himself to take it one day at a time.

Lily was not finished with her dad. She still had a lot more to say, "So, what are your plans for tonight, dad?"

"Well, I am taking my client to the theatre to see MAMMA MIA. She loves live theatre and, so do I.

"I know you do, dad," Lily said after a pause in the conversation. "Stay focused dad, remember this is purely business, nothing else."

She laughed into the phone, "You know what makes this even sweeter, dad. In the end Destiny is paying for all of it, you get to treat her with her own money.

It's a win-win for you dad." She laughed a bit more.

"Enjoy your evening nevertheless, and remember I love you. I will be back at the hotel tomorrow after lunch."

Lily was satisfied with what she'd heard from her dad. She was not planning on calling Destiny. Her dad was still alive and well and that was all that mattered to her.

She said goodbye and hung up the phone, not giving him a chance to respond.

Daniel hung the phone up, not pleased with some of the things Lily had said, but he could not let her break him, he had to hold it together because he knew what she was trying to do.

She was trying to put him on the defensive, and when he bites the bait by defending Destiny against her attacks, she would have him.

But he had news for his daughter – he has been a lawyer much longer than she has, and all that she knew, she'd learned from him.

He sighed, wondering why women were always competing with each other. He loved his daughter dearly, so he couldn't understand why she was so worried about Destiny. It seems so foolish to him, especially when he cares about both of them.

Destiny stirred something in him and last night he could not resist finding out what that something was.

He had started planning last night since before they arrived in London by taking better care of himself, dressing and smelling better; then after they arrived in London putting those plans into overdrive by booking a full package spa and salon appointment, hiring that personal shopper, making dinner reservations – requesting a table that gave him a view of the door so he could watch her as she did that seductive little sway she had as she walked in – a dozen roses, champagne, and the gold Cartier bracelet which reminded him of her and where he wanted them to be at first glance, all culminating in the explosion of exquisite chemistry that lit the night.

All along, he was aware he could lose his client if his plans failed, but it was a chance he had to take, because what he felt was real.

AN OFFICE AFFAIR

I discovered there was nothing Lily would not do to get what she wanted.

The woman, who to me, has everything, still believed she deserved more.

I came from the exact opposite end of her world, a world she knows nothing about and intended to keep it that way.

If I had not showed up with a ten-million-pound lottery ticket and started to move her dad's attention away from her, we would have never crossed path. But we did and here we are.

This new development in her life – meaning me - had only added to another problem Lily was already having, one she thought her dad knew nothing about, but she was wrong.

At dinner last night, Mr. Daly had confided in me that his daughter was having an office affair with one of the firm's partners, Mr. John Cramer.

Two weeks ago, John's wife Melissa came to Mr. Daily with proof of the affair. Melissa had paid one of the girls in the firm to snoop on her husband, and the girl came back with photos of them in various intimate positions on the desk in John's office. Those photos cost Melissa one thousand dollars and the girl, her job.

Melissa does not want a divorce. She is not interested in losing anything, what she wants is for Mr. Daly to find a way to stop his daughter from sleeping with her husband.

This was a tall order and Mr. Daly knew right away what had to be done. He'd confronted John and he admitted to the affair, apologized and promised that he would end it right away. He was also planning on having a similar talk with Lily, while they were in London.

A week ago, John had taken took a ten-day vacation away from the firm, with the excuse that he needed to clear his mind and mend fences. But Mr.

Daly believed that John had lied to him again; he was sure John was currently in London and Lily is with him, right this moment.

He knew that there was only one way to end the affair. Force John out of the firm. He has crossed the line and there was no coming back from this.

John Cramer is not planning on leaving his wife Melissa.

His wife is a beautiful woman, inside and out, she's sexy, and he has no problem sleeping with her. His problem as he sees it, is having a need to sleep with more than just her.

This is a problem he has been working on for many years, with no success, and he has come to accept it for what it is.

As much as he would like to believe that Daniel still trusted him, he could not help but wonder if he was planning to force him out of the firm.

Daniel always sat up there on his high horse, preaching to those he considers less than him, holding himself up as a beacon of virtue and respectability, John thought in distaste, a sneer curling his lips.

He knew that having an affair with Lily had crossed the line in more ways than one and that Daniel was going to make him pay for it.

But, if he was on his way out he was going to take some clients with him and right now Destiny Johnson and her ten million pounds was the prize.

He had given fifteen years to the firm and he was not about to let Lily and her Dad take everything away from him, nope, not for a decision that did not involve him alone.

He looked over at his accomplice, Lily, she was checking her email, oblivious that this was going to be the last of their illicit encounter in London, maybe forever. It was the end of an affair that she had no clue was coming.

John was lying in bed, watching her, planning his next moves.

It was not by choice that he was doing this, yet it had to be done. They had both made an unwise decision and now there was a price to pay.

Lily came to London to be with him, John was sure of that. Somehow, she had found a way to leave her dad and Destiny at the hotel when they arrived in London to come and spend time with him.

She has also been filling him in on everything that has been going on at the firm since he'd gone on vacation. She told him all about their new client, Destiny Johnson. She'd arrived at the law firm shortly before he'd taken his leave, the one that he was forced to take because of his affair.

He recalled how pleased his wife was when he told her that he was going off island for a while, no doubt happy that he would be away from the office and Lily.

He'd also lied to Daniel, only telling him a small part of the truth, enough to allow him to put his plan in action. He had promised to tell Lily that their affair was over before he left on a ten-day vacation, presumably to give her space and a chance to get over the breakup.

But John had no intention of telling Lily that; what he did tell her was that he was going to London for ten days to take care of some personal business. Shortly after he left, she updated him on the firm's new client. He knew every move they made, when and where in London they will be. They then planned their little sexual escapades around the Destiny Johnson business.

Now here he was, wondering what he should tell Lily before she leaves to take care of business, how much he should let her in on his plans, if at all.

Maybe he should have broached the subject before they took their clothes off, he thought for a second in hindsight, but discarded that thought quickly, knowing they would not have ended up in bed after that conversation. He decided to dive right in.

"Lily, your dad found out that you and I are having an affair," he said, interrupting her deep concentration, and watching as her dark head jerk up, green eyes widening.

"WHAT!" she shouted, "Are you insane, John? What the hell are you talking about?" Her mouth dropped open, a flicker of fear and confusion in her eyes.

"I said it because it's true, Lily. Stop acting like you didn't see this coming."

"See it coming, John?" she shouted again, a few decibels lower this time, as the color drained from her face, and her eyes glimmered with unshed tears.

She leapt off the bed, scrubbing at her eyes as she crossed to the window, smudging mascara and turning her back on him like it was his fault her dad was a nosy, self-righteous bastard.

"Come on, Lily, we're adults we can handle this."

"How John, can you tell me how we're going to handle this?" she said, swinging around to look at him. "Now my dad knows I was lying to him the whole time, and, he probably knows where I am right now."

"Maybe, but I did not tell him," John shot back. "I told him I was going away for ten days but I did not say I was going to London."

"No John, you don't get it, I insisted on coming to London with him and Destiny and to be perfectly honest, they don't need me here, they never did. Oh God, dad had to have suspected the real reason. He had to have known all along what I was up to. I lied right in his face."

"Oh, come on Lily, stop the theatrics, you are no angel."

"Shut up, John. Shut your stupid mouth!"

"So now I'm stupid?' John replied, raising an eyebrow in her direction.

Lily stalked over to the bed, grabbed a pillow and threw it at him in frustration. How did she not see this?

John ducked like a mere pillow was going to cause him irreparable harm in some way.

"You did this, John."

"Me?" he retorted, looking flabbergasted.

"Yes, you," she yelled, "you let me walk into this trap knowing damn well I was going to hang myself."

Lily paced up and down the hotel room, wondering what her dad must be thinking about her right now.

"My dad trusted me so much that next month when he retires I was going to take over the firm," she said, giving voice to her thoughts and concern.

"Is that so? Hmmm, interesting" John said, well, this he had already strongly suspected, but hey what the hell, he was willing to play along, and see what pops up.

"Well, where does that leave me, Lily?" He wanted to see who she thought was the real loser here in this little scenario of theirs, who should be crying, if either of them at all. Her true colors were showing now, not that he didn't already know that Lily was and would always be about Lily.

"Tell me John, how long since my dad knew about us."

"Almost three weeks ago," he replied, watching her intently but trying to appear nonchalant.

"And you are only now telling me, you selfish prick."

"Seriously, Lily, YOU think I'M selfish? Just because I did not tell you right away? Tell me, Lily, what you are about to lose from knowing this? Come on, tell me, name me one thing that you are about to lose. If anything, you are the selfish bitch here. Your dad loves you and he always will, oh sure he will be a little disappointed in you, but he will get over that, and do you want to know why?" he prompted, getting up out of bed to confront her.

"Because you are his daughter, his only child. Your name will always be on that law firm's door. You are all he has, and this affair, he will blame it all on me, and he will forgive you and trust you again. Do you understand that you lose nothing? I am the one who is going to lose here."

He did not say it was over between them, but that message was conveyed loud and clear. What he is sure of is that he will not be going back to the firm, he had enough information to take the new client away from them.

He just hoped Lily would not figure out why he had delayed telling her that her dad knew about them, but if she does, he will simply deny it. He had nothing to lose in that department.

He stormed out of the suite, slamming the door, not waiting for her response to his accusations, swearing to himself that he would never trust a Daly ever again.

Lily's ass did not need saving, his did.

He knew he could have broken the news a little kindlier, pretending he was devastated that their affair had been discovered and had to come to an end, but he was never good at playing the victim or playing by the rules.

He played to win, so, if breaking the rules helped him to win so be it.

She was as culpable as he was and must have known what the price of discovery was going to be.

He was certain that Daniel had not bought his promises to end the affair when he'd confronted him. He had to know that John was not going to go easily, resigning and just slinking quietly into the dark, his tail between his legs.

John fully intended to be at Camelot on Monday morning when the whole gang went to collect Destiny Johnson's winnings.

But it seemed like Daniel had a plan of his own.

This morning, he had sent a letter to John's hotel room, requesting his presence for lunch at the Mayfair hotel tomorrow. He knew that John was already in London, and likely spending time with his daughter.

The requested meeting was two hours after the one at Camelot, so it was safe to assume Daniel was planning to fire him after the firm had secured Destiny's lottery money.

John had no problem with this as his plan would be well executed by then.

Let's see whose client Destiny will be by noon on Monday. He was going to surprise yet another Daly in the next few hours.

He smiled and crossed his ankles as he leaned back against the elevator wall, time to surprise the leading ladies in his life right now.

A dozen, lovely red roses to his beautiful wife; he wanted her to know how much he missed her. Then a dozen pink carnations to his new client, welcoming her to the firm.

Lily was going to make John Cramer pay for trying to make a fool of her.

Luring her over to his hotel for three days to sleep with her then dumping her. Why did he wait so long to tell her? He must have something to gain from this.

What she had to do now was figure out why he did not tell her that her dad already knew about them, and what was it worth to him keeping this secret for so long. Was he trying to get even with her or was he trying to hurt her dad?

She was so occupied with Destiny that she failed to see what was right beneath her own nose.

She angrily shoved clothes and toiletries into her suitcase, she was not going to spend another minute under the same roof as John Cramer. If she did, one of them would be dead very soon.

She was going to call Michael to pick her up and take her back to The Mayfair Hotel where she will hide out in her room until tomorrow. She did not want to deal with her dad right now. Her life is such a mess right now, she was finding it hard to figure out how she had screwed up so badly.

All she wanted right now was comfort and a listening ear, not anger and condemnation; anyone who was oblivious to the mess she had made of her life would do just fine. Her mind thoughts turned to Jack, the one person who does not know anything about this mess.

A week ago, she was ready to leave him, yet here she was now, needing his love and comfort to make her feel whole again. She grabbed her cellular phone and punched in his number on the dial pad that was blurred by her tears, hoping it was not too late to save her marriage.

The ringing of the phone calmed her down a little. "Please answer the phone. I need you now more than ever," she whispered.

How could I have been so stupid, Lily thought, praying that Jack never finds out about her affair. He does not deserve it.

If her dad still thinks she is capable of handling the firm she will need to keep her marriage rock solid. Too many things were falling apart around them, and she knew they needed to keep Destiny as a client.

Her mental agony came to a screeching halt, as realization hit her. Maybe, just maybe, that's what John was after, and she had foolishly given him all the information he needed to try and steal her away from us! Oh My God!

She swore to herself that she was not going to let that happen, not if she can help it. Even though she did not like Destiny Johnson, all she was concerned with was making sure she remained their client. This is business and she was not about to lose anything.

Jack never answered, so Lily hung up the phone and dialed a taxi to take her back to the hotel.

MAMMA MIA!

I found a sexy little black dress.

A wool crepe blend, hugging all of my curves and resting four inches above the knees, showing just enough legs to tease. I topped it off with leather marigold pumps, and a grey wool blend coat and accessorized with crystal and gold earring, a soft grey and yellow clutch.

Let's not forget my lacy black push-up bra and matching panties. Hmm, it will be interesting to see just how long I will keep these two bits of cloth on tonight.

I am beginning to feel rich, just two days away from collecting it and the anticipation is already killing me.

Gone was that little girl from Blue Hills who had nothing but her older sisters' hand-me-downs to wear. It was a different world now.

My fragrance tonight is Chanel No. 5 and let's not forget the beautiful little Cartier bracelet Mr. Daly had bought me. What a lovely gift! When he told me what it meant last night, I could hardly believe it. I had definitely made an impression on him.

He even remembered every last detail of our first meeting, even as there were parts I would rather forget because I felt so out of my element. But what I saw as a gauche encounter, he recalled it as something entirely different, telling me that my heartfelt tears after we had confirmed my winnings was a tender moment that made him want to protect me. He even reminded me of that imperceptible bond we had shared, and which I was trying to ignore, when he'd moved closer and taken hold of my hand to calm me down.

I glanced down at the bracelet on my wrist, at the symbol of the two entwined hands, a reminder of the bond we shared.

Mr. Daly has definitely grown on me.

Later that night, after I'd gotten prepared, I took the lift down to the lobby to meet Mr. Daly. All the while fighting nervousness that had sprung up from nowhere.

What if Lily was waiting in the lobby? What would she think of my outfit?

This was not a business outfit, for sure. She would know that something was going on between her dad and I. Not that I know what that something really is, but I do know it was not about business tonight.

Dear God, when will I stop worrying about Lily? I scolded myself. It's almost as if Lily had found a way to seep into my pores and scare me shitless.

I shook off the nervousness, stuck my middle finger up in the air in defiance and waited for the elevator to get to the lobby, chanting to hell with Lily until it stopped at my destination.

As the door opened, I relaxed my hand and smiled. I'd finally found a way to banish her from my mind. I felt invigorated.

I stepped out of the elevator and there he was, my reason for being here.

Mr. Daly was looking so charming, the best dressed man in the Mayfair Hotel's lobby that evening.

Navy jacket accented with brown buttons comfortably encasing his frame, perfectly tailored khaki pants hugging his legs just enough to let you know that he is all man, set off by a blue pin stripe shirt with a beautiful burgundy necktie and brown leather shoes.

"Looks like someone went shopping," I said, smiling as I greeted him.

He reached for my hand and saw the bracelet, smiled and took his time surveying me from head to toe.

"You never disappoint me, my dear. I love it, all of it."

"Thank you," I purred, as he kissed me on the cheek.

"But, you, you look amazing," I said, mouth still dry and heart galloping a mile a minute, as I gestured at his ensemble.

I put my hands on my heart as if to slow it down. Wow! Words could not explain, I was speechless.

"My dear," he said smilingly, "I had a personal shopper come by my suite the day we arrived to help me look like this." He twirled for me, arms outstretched to give me a better view.

"Also," he continued, still modeling, "this afternoon I went to the hotel salon for a little trim here and there and this is what's left of me. Do you approve?"

"Yes, I most certainly do, sir," I promptly replied, smiling from ear to ear at his antics.

"You look smashing," I said and leaned in for another kiss.

"Are you ready to go, Destiny?

"Yes, I am."

He gestured for me to put my arm through his and we walked out of the hotel to our waiting car. Michael was already standing by the passenger side, opening the door when he spotted us.

"Good evening Sir! And um… Miss."

"Um, it's okay Michael," Mr. Daly said, no doubt seeing his confused and fascinated expression as his eyes lit on me.

It was obvious he was thrown off seeing us together, but I did not see the need to explain, couldn't even if I'd tried. Yet I could not help but wondering if Lily had told him to spy on us.

We got into the car and he drove away. We were having dinner before the theatre.

I turned to Mr. Daly, "You look so handsome tonight sir, what did you do with my lawyer?"

Mr. Daly looked at me then whispered in my ear, "I will show you later." We both smiled.

"I would love to know what you thought of last night, my dear. Maybe you can tell me over dinner," and this time he winked at me.

Are you sure you want to know what I thought," I said licking my lips.

"Well of course" he said. "Someone told me that the champagne was good, and the dessert was even better." Oh boy, so he wants to play, hmmm.

"Desert? Did we have desert last night?"

"Oh," he was smiling from ear to ear now. "Well, I remembered having dessert and it was mouthwateringly delicious."

So that's what he's calling it, ha. He licked his lips and I could feel my body immediately responding. Oh my god, I wonder if we were going to make it to dinner.

"My dear, I am hoping for more of that kind of dessert later. Would you care to join me?" Mr. Daly put his hand on my thigh, the electric shock of his hands sizzling through the fabric right, into the core of me. I had to look away and out at the vehicles speeding by. I needed to distract myself.

Michael pulled up at the curb shortly after, just in time to save the remaining scraps of my senses. He quickly jumped out of the car, then open my door with a flourish, cheerily announcing, "Dinner Time."

I stepped out, smiling at him, but he avoided my eyes. I wondered if I had done something wrong to him, then lightly shrugged, it surely did not matter now, did it.

Mr. Daly got out and politely asked Michael to be back here in one and a half hour. Michael nodded his head in agreement, then he side-eyed me.

We walked proceeded to the restaurant, but soon as we were out of sight of anyone, he pulled me close to him and just held me, breathing deeply. I could feel his heart beating rhythmically against my chest. I felt safe.

I looked up at his handsome face and my desire melted into his, as he touched the sides of my face then allowing his fingers to lightly trace the shape of my lips. I opened them slightly, responding to his touch, allowing him entry. He stared at me, and I leaned into him, kissing him gently.

"Are you hungry? He finally spoke.

I nodded yes.

"Let's go inside and have dinner."

It has been years since I'd been to a live performance, and right now I could not imagine a better person with whom I wanted to be there.

We had purchased balcony seats; a little pricey, but worth it.

Apropos of nothing, Mr. Daly blurted out, "Did you notice I have not had a drink of whisky since I arrived in London?"

"Well," I said, a bit surprised, "I have not checked the mini bar in your suite."

"And neither have I," he replied.

I think I knew where this was going. He wanted to have a whisky, and for some reason was asking permission from me. A little odd, I thought, but I was okay with it.

"Would you like to have one now?"

"No darling, I just wanted to see if you were paying attention."

"Well," I said, "I am paying attention more than you know." Mr. Daly has had my undivided attention ever since we arrived in London.

Sitting here in the theatre with him and hearing him asking me this made me more aware of how much closer we were becoming, but I did not tell him that, instead I said, "Lily would be happy to hear that you have not had any whisky since you arrived. Have you heard from her?"

"Yes, I did darling. Lily called me this afternoon, wanting to know if I was sober and on my best behavior." He kissed my hands then added, "Sober enough to remember that I made passionate love to you last night and again this afternoon."

Shocked and horrified I pulled my hand away, "You told her that?"

"Told her what?"

"What you just said to me," I spot back.

"No, I did not tell her that, my dear. I am just telling you," he said, then seeing the fear in my eyes, he continued, "Please, no, I did not say that to her. Darling, I will not do anything to spoil what we have right now, and I am sorry if I scared you. That was not my intention." He put his arm around me and gently pulled me into him.

"It's okay," I said, beginning to feel a little silly. "I don't quite know what it is, Mr. Daly, but just hearing Lily's name makes me nervous. She doesn't like me, but…"

"I do," he interrupted, "I like you a lot, and one day she will understand that." He kissed me on the forehead, "Let's watch the show."

But I couldn't, as worry gnawed away at me, making me edgy and unable to concentrate on the show.

Things once thought forbidden were now spinning out of control - like Mr. Daly and I. We had definitely crossed the line and neither of us had mentioned it as yet. How did this happen? I never thought I would end up in bed with my lawyer. But as much as I tried to make myself regret it, I couldn't, so I willed the thoughts away telling myself that the here and now was all that mattered, even if the feeling did not last.

I knew this was more than a little irresponsible, but I was not in the mood to think straight, I had to get away from these thoughts for a moment, so I excused myself to go the ladies' room.

I sat in the restroom stall trying not to think of what I was doing, or how wrong it might be. Leave me alone, I deserve happiness, but my subconscious shot right back with, this is not happiness, this is selfishness.

I was riddled with guilt, and as the tears began to flow, I felt no better than Lily, wanting it all no matter the cost.

I did not realize how long I was gone until I heard Mr. Daly's voice, "Are you okay in there, darling?" startling me up out of the chair.

"Yes, I am, be out in a minute." I said, lightly patting the tears away so as not to smudge my makeup, then applying a little bit of lipstick and powder to erase all signs of tears.

When I walked out, Mr. Daly was still standing by the door to the ladies, I gave him a bright smile and we walked hand in hand back to our balcony seats. When we got there, I ordered a glass of champagne to further fortify myself.

"Make that two glasses of champagne," Mr. Daly told the server, before we settled in to enjoy the rest of the show.

When it was over, we strolled around the West End of London, and just like he promised, he was my tour guide.

The night wind was so brisk, I felt myself shivering a few times under my coat, thankful for the warmth it provided.

As our tour progressed, I began to space out just a bit as worry seeped back into my consciousness.

Sensing that something was a little off, no doubt from my continued silence, Mr. Daly suggested that we head back to the hotel and warming conditions.

When Michael picked up us up, I was happy for the warmth of the car. I leaned my head on Mr. Daly's shoulder and closed my eyes.

We were quiet the whole ride back.

When we arrived at the hotel, he walked me to my suite, then suggested we have a drink before turning in for the night. He wanted to make sure I was okay before he left me. I nodded, and he rang room service for a bottle of champagne before leaving for his own suite to change into warmer clothing.

I wanted to change into something warm. My mind was miles away as I changed into the plush cream color terry cloth bathrobe provided by the hotel. I pulled it close to my body, burrowing into its soft warmth.

This was not the sexiest look, but it sure was warm and comfortable.

I sank into one of the chairs, legs curled up under me. It's like I was looking for protection and comfort from the robe and the chair.

It was Saturday night, and I thought of planning my Sunday. Wait a minute, I looked at the clock in my suite and the time is actually 12:10am Sunday morning. It was already Sunday, one more day and I will have my money. The thought cheered me up.

Wait a minute, where did I put my ticket? Focus, I told myself. If I lose it, I lose everything as I definitely won't be able to claim my money without that ticket.

I went back into the safe deposit box and removed everything, searching thoroughly. Then it occurred to me where I'd put it last. I flipped through the pages of my passport that I'd just pulled out of the safe, and there it was, my lottery ticket.

I held it tightly in my hand, being careful not to tear it, as I thought of the freedom it signified. As I replaced it in its hiding place, I decided that tomorrow on my way to Camelot it will be in my bra, that way no one can take it away from me.

CHEERING UP

As I was closing the safe, I heard a knock on my door. I was already feeling much better, so I decided to set the mood.

I quickly found a soft jazz channel on the television, Kenny G with the most appropriate song for the moment as I dimmed the lights and opened the door to my suite.

The melodic opening instrumental of Kenny G's 'End of the night' had just filled my suite when Mr. Daly walked in, wearing his own terrycloth bathrobe, a bottle of champagne swaying gayly in his hand. Our moods had both lifted, that much was obvious.

He looked me over, smiled, "You look happy."

"I know," I said, "I am happy, it just occurred to me that it's Sunday morning."

"Is it?" he quipped.

"Yes lover" I winked, and giggling glanced over to the clock to make sure I hadn't misread the first time. "It's now twelve-thirty on Sunday morning."

"Okay, and that's important to you because?" he leaned in to me like he was trying to capture every syllable as it passed my lips.

"Well," I breathed, "because tomorrow, Monday morning I will be claiming my ten-million-pound lottery win."

"Yes," he yelled suddenly", "now darling, that is definite cause to celebrate, don't you think?" Pouring champagne into the two flutes he'd grabbed from the desk.

He handed me my glass and I said, "Absolutely. Cheers!"

The champagne flowed as we sat there together, engrossed in each other, lightly flirting and giggling like teenagers. Suddenly he got a little serious, watching me intently, as I got up to dance in the middle of the suite.

"I love you, darling," he said quietly.

I felt it was the champagne talking, but I still wanted to respond with "Me too", instead I smiled and reached out to him to join me.

My anticipation of Monday morning was bubbling up inside, along with the champagne and the serenity of the moment. I was one day away.

He got up, taking hold of my hand and swayed with me.

"Thank you," I said.

"For what?" he asked. "I should be the one thanking you, darling. It's because of you I'm here, that we are here together. You are a dream."

I went quiet in his arms, but he continued, "The last two weeks my whole life has changed so much, and because of you I am now full of gratitude. I love every minute of this. I'd spent the last five years fighting to find reasons to carry on until you walked into my office."

He paused, then, "Come let's sit, darling."

We sat down on the coach in my suite. I almost forgot the music was playing, I was so attuned to him, everything else was just background noise.

"I know you see me as a man with everything, and truth be told I have been very fortunate in my life. I have built that law firm to what it is today, and I am very proud of my accomplishment there. I am even more proud of my daughter Lily and her ability to run the firm without me being there full time.

"In a month's time, I am going to retire, and this is something I was looking forward to.

"What I am saying Destiny is that I no longer feel needed. Lily can run the firm without me, but she drags me in there, just to keep an eye on me. I am glad she forced me in two weeks ago when I met you. I was not looking nor feeling my best, but something magical happened."

He stared into my eyes as if by force of will alone, he could make me believe every word he was about to say, "Darling, you make me feel alive and needed, and that is more than I can hope for at this age. My dear, this is a dream come true."

The words had barely escaped his lips when I kissed him, gently.

I climbed into his lap, wrapping my arms around his neck and just looked at him.

He wasn't done. "You captivate me, darling. Something stirred in me when I first saw you."

I buried my head in his neck, murmuring, "You're going to make me cry, shh..." I put my finger on his lips than I stood up to loosen my robe and pour us some more champagne.

I sat back down on his lap and made a toast, "Here's to finding each other."

I'm not sure I could follow up what Mr. Daly had said to me earlier, I could barely string words together into coherent sentences.

I could not lie to him right now, and at the same time, I was not entirely sure that any of this was real. It felt like a fantasy, or a dream that I was going to wake up from.

I struggled to stay focus on the real reason I was in London. The one I was sure about. Maybe my lawyer is seducing me? Well, technically he has already, but, I was not sure how okay I was talking about what had transpired between us and what was still going on, and here he was trying to explain what he was feeling. But I could not go there, I had to stay focused on what was ultimately important, which tonight was the way he was making my body tingle, not romantic feelings of love. I silently pleaded with him to lose the words, not to make me say something I can't live up to.

Probably hearing my silent plea, he remained quiet as he reached for my almost naked body, standing me up in front of him and burying his head in my stomach as his arms wrapped around my waist and his lips caressed me with sweet soft kisses.

He took one of his arms from around me, using it to remove my robe and his. I kissed him passionately as he lifted me, carrying me over to the bed.

As he laid my naked body on the warm sheets, his mouth soon followed, then his body, encasing me in his warmth as he urgently joined our bodies together in sweet ecstasy, and for the next hour we explored the depths of our desires with no regrets.

"I have to leave you, darling," Mr. Daly said.

It was 3am Sunday morning and he was afraid he won't wake up before lunchtime.

"What is happening at lunchtime?" I asked sleepily.

Have you forgotten already? He said. "Do you really want me to remind you of this right now, after all of this? Go back to bed darling, we can talk about this at dinner tonight."

"And spoil my dinner? I don't think so," I said, coming awake a little more.

"Okay, remember you asked for it, Destiny. Lily is coming back to the hotel today."

"Well, I do see the fear in that sir," I said sarcastically.

"I am not afraid of Lily, darling you are," he responded.

"So, you are leaving my suite because you are afraid for me?

Daniel was not ready to fight, he just wanted to go to his suite quietly. He knew Lily was a sore subject for Destiny, and after such a beautiful evening talking about her was not the way he wanted to end their time together.

"Let's get some more sleep, okay. I am sure at dinner tonight we will both be in a better position to understand what I am about to do. I am leaving now, and I am going to my suite. I will call you later this afternoon, after my meeting with Lily," he smiled, adding, "sleep well my dear."

Destiny watched him leave, now fully awake. She felt like she was now seeing her lawyer for the first time since they arrived in London. He had just made a complete 180 degrees on her, making her feel like the dream that was the last few days was now over. It was time for business.

She did not get a goodbye kiss. She wondered if she had done something to upset him. Was he displeased that I did not reciprocate when he declared his feelings for me last night? Or was it about Lily? She has a way of stealing the moment.

I felt like the train just pulled into the station, and I was asked to get off but I'm not sure where I am. Mr. Daly has left and now I'm not sure where that left us.

Daniel tossed and turned in his own bed, urging sleep to come so he could get a few more hours in before his day started.

But sleep was elusive.

It was after 4:00am Sunday morning and he had three pressing issues on his mind. None of them had to do with the reason he came to London in the first place. Before he arrived in London he had it all figured out how he was going to ask John Cramer to leave the firm then he was going to have a talk with his daughter about how disappointed he was in her behavior, and if she denied it he had proof. The photos of her and John that Melissa had given to him.

He had his firm to think about and Lily's reputation, but now he has compounded this whole sordid situation with his own ethical violation, becoming like the people he was getting ready to admonish.

He knew he was fooling himself by thinking that his actions were any different from theirs because of the fact that unlike them, he was not married. But he knew he was violating his own moral code of never becoming involved with a client, and now that he has to confront Lily and John, his conscience is pricking him.

He now knows that to make this right he too had to stop what he was doing with Destiny. He knows what he feels for her, and more so now that he had allowed champagne and sex to overwhelm him.

He had said things to Destiny that he should not have, even though at the moment he meant all of it.

But in light of what was happening between Lily and John, he too would have to make some changes.

What a pickle this entire situation was, he grunted in frustration, tossing the covers off of him. Damn, they have all lost their minds.

Lily will be taking over the firm in a month, this was a fact. They have been discussing her ascendancy for over a year and in that time, she has proven that she was more than capable. She had been so proud and happy when I'd first suggested it, probably assuming that John would have been the one to take over when he retires. After all, he had been at the firm much longer than her, fifteen years to be exact and John knew things about the law and the firm that she was just finding out. John had taken her under his wing when she first joined the firm, teaching her the ropes. But it's clear now that he was doing more than just mentoring, and this was unacceptable, not just because they were both married, but office romances were strictly forbidden, as the firm's code of ethic handbook clearly outlines.

"What could have possessed Lily," he thought in annoyance. Something has definitely changed in her. They used to be so close, talking every day on the phone, and sometimes she would stop by his house after work if he hadn't gone in that day, just to update him on their work. She would talk about a difficult client, a pressing case, or just ask his opinion about what he would have done in a particular situation.

Daniel had lost a lot of interest in the law after having practiced for three decades, but Lily refused to let him retire fully before the age of sixty-five.

Whenever she came over, she would pour herself a drink and sit down in what used to be her mother's favorite recliner chair and pick his brain.

She reminded him so much of himself, twenty years younger and hungry for knowledge of the law.

He treasured those moments with his daughter, because when Lily married Jack after her mother died, he thought he was losing her too.

He was not exactly thrilled at her choice in husband, thinking that Jack was not her equal, even though he was a good man. He was not ambitious enough for Lily, he did not have that drive that she had inherited from her father.

John Cramer on the other hand would have been the perfect match for her five years ago. They are both lawyers, and both driven and ambitious, but John was married.

This last fact made Daniel think less of him, given his recent escapades with his daughter. John had to go, there was no doubt about this. He was going to ask him to resign from the law firm.

He knew that Lily was not blameless; she had irritated him with her terrible lapse in judgement, but she is still his flesh and blood.

He will have to sit her down and read her the riot act, not only about her affair, but also about some of the suggestions she made to him concerning their new client. Those suggestions still made him extremely uncomfortable.

Lily had suggested that Destiny's winnings be transferred into the firm's account, then we wait a month or two before we formed a company for her.

She'd said, "Dad, do you know the kind of interest we will earn on that money?"

I was dumbfounded. "Lily, are you serious? You can't just take all of her money like it's yours."

"We are not taking it, dad. We are holding it until we form her company, and, in the meantime, we make a profit. She will still get all of her money."

Daniel was not comfortable with this suggestion, saying, "The money does not belong to the firm, Lily, it belongs to our client and she should decide where her money goes. Furthermore, I am sure she is aware that her money would gain interest if it sits in a savings or an investment account."

"You think she would know, dad," Lily said, smirking, "Come on, dad she is not smart like us. Since when did you start caring so much about your client? She is not your lover, she is your client and we are in business to make money."

"To earn it, Lily, not steal it," Daniel admonished her.

"Oh, so you think she earned it?"

"Well, she damn well did not steal it, Lily," he said, worried at her reasoning.

"She got lucky, dad."

"And is that a crime, Lily?"

"Dad, come on, you know what I'm saying."

No, I don't know what you're saying," Daniel fairly shouted back at her, finally tired of the discussion. "What has gotten into you lately?

"Dad, you spent so much money educating me in order to give me the best chance to succeed in life, you spent thirty years building your law firm, you put in the time. Think about it, we did everything society asked of us, but do we have ten million pounds?"

What is wrong with her, Daniel wondered. "Is that what this is about, Lily? You feel you deserve this more than Destiny? If you really feel that way, then why don't you take a chance and buy a damn lottery ticket like she did? She is not privileged like you, Lily. And yes, you're right, she does not have the education you have, and I am sure the thought has occurred to her that we would come up with a way to screw her out of her money, just like you are asking me to do right now. You are behaving like a spoiled, privileged brat and I am not going to countenance this kind of behavior."

Well, let's be honest here dad," an unperturbed Lily replied. "No one wants to screw her more than you do right now. How about that for honesty?"

He shook his head now, wondering if he was that obvious, even then. He definitely had some damage control to do today at lunch, but right now he needed to relax his mind and get some more sleep because he is not sure how much sleep he will get after today.

God help him.

SPY GAMES

Michael was scheming.

Four days ago, when he picked up his new clients from the airport, he had been recruited to do something he wasn't sure he could do, but he needed the money.

Now, he was being summoned to dinner at the May Fair hotel to deliver a status report.

Lily was back from her three day trip and she wanted to know exactly what had happened between Destiny Johnson and her dad while she was away. Information she had paid five thousand pounds for, all of which he still had as he was not able to fulfill her demands.

She had hired him to spy on them for her but before he could say yes or no to the job, she'd put the envelope on the car seat and left. In that envelope was the cash and instructions. He was instructed to take photos as proof and to record days and times they were together, but what she wanted most was for there to be no physical contact between the two of them.

Was she insane, he'd thought going down the list of demands. How was he supposed to stop physical contact between them if that is what they wanted?

But she had clearly thought this through, as at the end of her list, Lily suggested something that blew him away.

She'd written that Destiny has a crush on him, that she was a cougar – liked younger men. She then went on to describe Destiny's reaction to him when he'd picked them up at the airport, suggesting that he take advantage of her attraction and seduce her.

Michael could not believe what he was reading - for five thousand pounds, he was being asked to jeopardies his job by seducing a woman he did not know, by another woman he did not know.

He could sure use the money, but he was not sure if he could fulfill that last demand.

He knew the art of romance, that was easy, especially with his good looks, but he wasn't sure he was willing to work his charm on a woman who was probably old enough to be his mum.

At thirty-five years old, he liked his women younger. Lily looked around his age, and he thought that if he had to be with a woman older than his preference, it would be her.

Maybe Lily had read the signs wrong, and Destiny was not as into him as she described. She could tell him to go to hell, or worse, tell the old man about it.

Then, he would definitely lose his job.

The more he thought about it, the more he realized that he could not do this, not even for five thousand pounds. He has his standards and the risk was definitely not worth the reward.

He wondered why Destiny was such a problem to Lily, she hadn't said, or given him a chance to ask.

He'd read the list and counted the money a lot in the last three days, but he could not find a way to fulfill her wishes. The thoughts were stressing him out, and because of that, he felt he deserved to keep the money, so that was exactly what he planned to do, even if it meant fabricating a story to tell her.

The few times he'd seen Destiny she was always accompanied by old man Daly, and she looked happy in his company.

There was no room for seducing her, even if he wanted to, because clearly old man Daly had taken care of that part. She looked really into Daly.

Maybe she likes them old, Daly was clearly much older than her, and as far as Michael had seen, irrespective of what Lily thought she'd seen, Destiny was not attracted to him, she had barely even noticed him.

Now he wondered how he was going to go about convincing Lily of whatever it is she needed convincing of, so he could keep the cash. She had been quick to point out that she and her dad were both lawyers, not mentioning anything about Destiny's profession. Maybe she was the secretary or the old man's mistress.

Whoever she was, Lily was determined to keep them apart; that's why her leaving them alone didn't make any sense. What could have been more important to her than this, that she was willing to pay a stranger five thousand pounds to do what she could easily do on her own for free?

Michael was not looking forward to seeing Lily later for dinner.

Lily hung up the phone.

She had just made plans for dinner tonight with the driver, now it was time to have lunch with her dad.

She frowned at the thought of having to sit through lunch with her dad after what John told her yesterday. She wondered what he was thinking about their affair and her.

She had lied to him about spending the past three days with friends from law school.

She now remembered how he did not give much of a reply when she'd said it. He had appeared distracted, making it easy for her to get away with the lie. She'd wondered if he were distracted because he was up to something with Destiny. That is why she had hired Michael to spy on them.

But now she knows that her dad was on to her all along. He knew of her affair and he knew she was lying when she told him that she was going to be with her old friends from law school.

Well, she sure hoped Michael had something for her, something she could use against her dad and Destiny. Something that would help her look better than she is looking right now, if that's possible.

She had arrived back at the hotel last night early enough to have dinner with her dad, but she was not in the mood to see him just yet.

Days ago, he had mentioned that he was taking their client to dinner and the theatre. Now she was a little happy about that, she was off the hook, and she was not in the mood for Destiny's company either.

She had needed some time alone to come up with a plan for damage control after the information John had blindsided her with.

She was still upset about all of it – the deception and how he had just blurted it out like it was nothing to him. He can be so insensitive at times.

She felt disappointed by him and she wondered if what they shared meant anything to him at all.

She knew he had to have been plotting all along on how to leave the firm with something of value, Lily was sure of that; and she might have helped him indirectly.

He wanted Destiny as a client to take with him when he leaves the firm, and she was not going to let that happen.

Neither was she going to accept being used and then unceremoniously dumped.

After all that they had shared, he could have been gentler. His behavior was unforgivable, and her feelings were hurt. What made it worst was that he had called her a selfish little bitch.

Now here she was left with having to face her dad after lying to him.

She decided that she was going to skip lunch altogether.

101

He dad didn't know that she had arrived back at the hotel last night, so he was actually expecting her back at a little after noon today.

She decided that she was going to ring him at two o'clock and say that she'd just arrived at the Mayfair and was too tired, then suggest they meet at five after she had taken a nap. Then at five she will call with another lie, saying that she'd forgotten a dinner date that evening that she could not get out of.

This way, she can avoid having that uncomfortable confrontation until after their meeting tomorrow at Camelot with Destiny.

With that plan tucked away, she relaxed, prepared to have a lazy Sunday, free of drama, then have dinner with Michael.

Come to think of it, maybe seeing Michael tonight might help her tremendously when she comes face to face with her dad again.

CALM

Islept through breakfast and lunch.
When I finally woke up it was mid-afternoon, and it occurred to me that this was the first time I'd woken up in my suite alone since arriving in London.

I didn't mind that much because I needed some alone time to prepare for tomorrow, the day I was looking forward to for the past two weeks.

I did not want to think about anything else.

Sinking back into the plush pillows, I sucked in the stillness, the small whisper of sounds and music that occupied each day - distant chatter, the muted sounds of horns that filtered into the room from the slightly opened window.

I lay there listening, feeling very present, hoping for nothing in particular but just wanting to be still.

Peace had finally arrived, right here in my luxurious suite, in the heart of London. I closed my eyes and felt myself drifting into the vast space of nothingness, feeling like I was being welcomed into a whole new world.

I stepped into it gracefully, into where there was no beginning or ending, just a renewed sense of life that was beautiful and peaceful.

I floated on clouds of happiness, wanting nothing more from life in that moment.

Dear God, my subconscious whispered into the nothingness, thank you for hearing me all those years ago when I knelt in prayer to you. I didn't think you would give me a dream too big to be fulfilled. Thank you for fulfilling it, thank you for trusting me with it, thank you for instilling in me the wisdom, the understanding and the faith to lean on you. To trust in your divine plan, to trust in your divine order, to trust in your divine timing.

Thank you for the blessing that you have bestowed upon me. God, help me to remain grounded through all the changes that are taking place in my life. Show up for me tomorrow like never before as my new journey begins and remind me that you are with me always.

"Amen," I whispered, as tears wet my cheeks.

Thump! Thump!

I jerked up, did someone just knock on the door to the suite?

I was still in a bit of a fog after saying my prayer. Who could it be? Who could be so presumptuous as to come over without calling first? I was not expecting anyone, not even Mr. Daly.

Maybe it was Lily, but I shook off that thought, no, it can't be her. She would sooner send a messenger than come knocking herself, anything to avoid having to be nice to me.

But who could it be really?

It took me a minute to roll out of bed and put on some clothes, check my face and hair in the mirror before opening the door, knowing I did not look my best.

There was no one there.

I poked my head out the door, looking up and down the corridor, no one was in sight. Maybe I was hearing things, but I didn't really think so. There was a knock on the door.

I stepped back, pulling my head back into the room, about to close the door, when I finally looked down. Lying on the carpeted floor was a large vase of pink carnations.

At that moment, I thought it did not matter how I looked because nothing could possibly be prettier than the sight in front of me.

I bent down and scooped up the vase, a huge smile splitting my face from ear to ear.

As I closed the door behind me, I wondered what exactly I'd done to deserve this beautiful, unexpected present. Was it the prayer?

Still not able to take my eyes off the flowers, I put the vase on the desk and sat down in front of it in awe. Someone was really thinking about me today.

Those beautiful pink carnations captured my attention so much, I could almost feel the love coming from it. It could only be Mr. Daly. No one in London knows me that well or even cared about me that much to send me flowers, no one else but him.

Oh my god, I thought in sudden awe, maybe those words were real. Those words of love he shared last night after having too much champagne.

He'd really meant it. It was not the alcohol speaking after all, or the anticipation of the moment, he really does care for me.

Maybe I was reading too much into this, besides, as sweet as it was, I'm not sure I'm ready for any of this, and I definitely did not want to read what was written in the card either.

I closed my eyes, covering my face with the card in my hands, trying not to think about it and reaching for my calm again. How could I lose it so quickly?

Thankfully, the phone rang.

I put down the card and answered the phone. Mr. Daly's voice came through the lines, loud and clear. A part of me was happy, while another part was not too keen to speak to him right now.

He wanted to know if I'd gotten some more rest, and if I could join him for dinner tonight. Lily had cancelled on him. I heard him but wondered why he didn't bring up the carnations; maybe he was waiting for me to thank him for the beautiful flowers and the lovely words, even though I haven't read it as yet.

"Destiny, are you there? Are you okay?" He was still waiting for a response to his dinner invitation.

I could not do it, no, I did not want to do it because I knew how the evening was going to end, and I wanted to be by myself tonight. "Thanks for the dinner invitation, Mr. Daly, but I think I will pass on this evening. I need some time alone tonight, to prepare for tomorrow." I hung up the phone before he had a chance to answer or change my mind.

I sat there for a moment, telling myself that I had done the right thing, still trying to regain the calmness I'd felt on waking.

But that was not about to happen anytime soon, because next to the phone was the card. I picked it up and examined it; it was not from Mr. Daly. It was from John Cramer.

Suddenly my heart started racing as my brain scrambled to make sense of it of why he would be sending me flowers. I've never met the man and all that I've heard about him so far was not good.

The card read, 'Hello Destiny, let me take this time to welcome you to the firm. Looking forward to meeting you tomorrow before our appointment at Camelot. Cheers, John Cramer."

Wait, what? Did I have an appointment tomorrow with John Cramer at Camelot?

I don't think so. Last I'd heard of him he was leaving the firm because Mr. Daly was going to force him to resign. What is he trying to do?

I threw the card back away from me, watching it fall to the floor, then glanced back up at the beautiful carnations.

I sighed in annoyance and frustration, this did not bode well. Since answering that mysterious knock at the door, everything seemed to be conspiring to rob me of newfound peace, and I had a bad feeling about this new development.

One day away from my big moment and now this – Mr. Daly's soon to be ex-partner, whom I had never met – was sending me flowers and confirming an appointment he was never invited to as far as I was aware.

I wondered if I should call back Mr. Daly and let him know about this, and maybe Lily needed to know as well. I was sure they would know why he is doing this, because right now I couldn't figure it out on my own.

I was also ready to put that beautiful vase of flowers back where I'd found it, right along with the offending card. Maybe then I can pretend I'd never received it.

This seemed a better solution than telling either of them; if I told them it would probably create another problem, derailing the rest of my afternoon, the very last thing I wanted right now.

I wanted my afternoon back, the one I'd woken up to before I'd opened the door, just one more day of peace before my life officially changed. Course of action decided, I picked up the phone and called room service to order some food and enough booze to keep me happy until tomorrow.

THE FAX

Daniel stared down at a fax that was just sent to him from his law firm in Providenciales, Turks and Caicos.

He had been expecting the document to read that Ms. Destiny Johnson now has a company registered in her name and the account number of that company where her lottery winnings would be deposited tomorrow. But the document in front of him read everything but that.

What the hell was going on? Lily had assured him that the company's registration and opening of an account in the company's name could be done in time for tomorrow's meeting.

Daniel knew that these sorts of things usually take up to one month, but the firm had connections that would have expedited the process for an extra thousand dollars, all within three days.

He was sure Lily had received all of the necessary documents from Grand Turk, the capital of Turks and Caicos.

He clearly remembered her saying to him the day they left for London that she had taken care of everything. That was good enough for him, so he'd left things in her capable hands as he had to take care of another job – that of ensuring that Destiny had the ticket with her before they left the airport in Providenciales.

He'd asked her, and she appeared delighted to let him know that the lottery ticket was in a very safe place somewhere on her body.

He remembered being very interested in knowing just where on her body was that lucky ticket.

But now that his job was done, he's only now finding out that the company was not registered as yet and won't be for another two or more weeks.

Knowing how slow and unreliable doing business is in the Islands, he had only one choice left, to put Destiny's money into the firm's account just like Lily had suggested.

As soon as the idea came to him he saw the real picture. This had to be Lily's doing, it was not a mistake, it was planned.

He had to take a deep breath to calm himself, before taking the next step and accusing his daughter of lying to him about everything - about forming the company, where she's been the last three days and God knows what else.

There had to be more to this.

He knew that he had strayed away from the real reason they were in London by getting caught up in his feelings for Destiny, so he felt responsible in part for this latest mess.

When he should have been double and triple checking on the business end of things, making sure everything was in order and ready for tomorrow, he had instead been romancing and seducing.

But the only thing that mattered now was finding a way to make this right. He was already concerned about looking shady to Destiny and he'd already crossed the line by getting intimate with her, now this.

What was she going to think about him when he tells her this? Daniel sighed.

Lily was already ten minutes late getting to the business center for the meeting they had planned for five-thirty.

The one he asked her to make after she'd cancelled on their dinner plans.

He needed to talk to her before breakfast tomorrow morning.

Where the hell was she? Daniel thought, looking around the room.

Before he confronted her about the fax, he was going to discuss her affair with John. He'd brought along the photographs Melissa had given to him. He'd taken one look before he was disgusted. There they were, making out on John's desk like two horny teenagers. Right under his nose, in his own law firm they had managed to carry on without him knowing. They must have thought him an old fool.

But there is a price to pay for behaving like this, and someone was going to pay that price, he was going to make sure of it.

But that had to wait because he had to figure out a way to still be Destiny's lawyer tomorrow morning.

He had phoned Destiny around four o'clock to ask if she would join him for dinner tonight after Lily had cancelled on him for a dinner date she said she had made with their driver Michael.

Before he could ask what that was about, she'd launched into a long explanation about how Michael was in desperate need of some legal advice and she'd offered her service for free if he paid for dinner.

The explanation didn't make much sense, but he didn't force the issue because he was relieved she was not having dinner with John, even though having dinner with their driver was not typical Lily. Maybe she was finally learning some humility.

He was excited at the prospect of seeing Destiny that evening even if he was not sure it would go beyond dinner. He wanted to make sure that things were okay between them regardless of where their fledgling relationship went after their business in London was over.

He was here on business and he was ready to take care of that and only that, if that was what she wanted. Judging by her rejection of his invitation, that was indeed what she wanted.

After this meeting with Lily he was going to have dinner alone for the first time since he'd arrived in London. The prospect of which made him long for his old friend – whisky - even more so after that fax he'd just received.

Lily walked into the business center twenty minutes late and well aware of it.

She saw her dad looking down at his watch when he spotted her, indicating that he too was aware of her tardiness.

She had been rehearsing how she was going to control the conversation, it was to be about business and nothing else. There will be no discussion about the affair.

No, not tonight!

She loved her dad and she was going to remind him of why he loved her and depended on her, then they were going to discuss their ten million pounds client and make sure that everything was in order for their arrival at Camelot tomorrow.

Just thinking about it made her excited. She would have her seal written all over this contract, and next month, she would be in charge of the law firm and Destiny's money.

She was going to prove to her dad once and for all that he had made the right choice when he chose her over John Cramer to run the firm. Lily knew that she was lucky when he decided to hand her the reins to his legacy. John had more experience than her, but she was Daniel Daly's daughter, making her the better choice to carry on his legacy.

She, better than anyone, understood the importance and pride her dad took in the Daly name, in the sweat and blood that he had poured into the firm to make it into what it is today.

She was already taking care of business, and in just a few more minutes her dad would understand and thank her for it.

She was more than amply prepared for tonight and looking like the lady in charge.

She'd decided to channel her softer feminine side tonight, donning a dress instead of a pants suit. She had at least two male companions to impress.

Her floral dress hung close to her slender frame, stopping just below her knees. This dress made her look younger and more approachable. Burgundy pumps added three inches to her height and showed off her beautiful legs, legs that had just delivered her beside her dad's table.

"Hi dad, sorry I'm late." She leaned over him and kissed him on his right cheek, smiled into his eyes then added, "I love you daddy."

Lily sat down next to her dad, placing a hand on his back and gently massaged muscles that felt knotted in tension.

"How are you dad?" she asked innocently, still massaging.

"I am… well, I am not sure right now," he replied, wondering what her scheme was. He knew she had a plan to wiggle her way out from under the mess that was before them.

She was trying to calm him, but she was also trying to confuse him at the same time.

"What is going on, Lily?"

"What do you mean, dad?"

"Well, for one you come in here all dressed up like…" he paused, "…like a lady, all feminine and looking pretty? Is that what you are trying to say, dad?"

"Well, I am going on a date, remember I told you earlier."

He remembered, and he was going to remind her of something else. "What is his name again? Michael, right? Well, don't forget to tell Michael about your husband Jack Shaw."

"It's not like that, dad. Believe me."

Right now, he was finding it hard to believe anything she had to say, but he knew he had to listen.

"Sorry dad, but I don't have much time to sit and catch up. We have to discuss the business at hand, our client Destiny." Her hand stopped the calming movements on his back.

"Lily," he said when she paused for a breath, "I am going to ask you one question and I want a simple answer. Did you form the company for Destiny, yes or no?"

Lily knew that the shit was about to hit the fan, and she also knew that her dad already knew the answer to that question.

She wished he could see how this is going to work in their favor and just get over it. She had already explained all of this to him before, so why is he doing this to her now.

"Did you form the company for Destiny?" he repeated.

"Dad, you already know the answer to that question," she said.

"Which is?" he replied.

Lily was beginning to lose control of the situation and it was showing. She was biting down on her bottom lip, hard. "What do you want me to say, dad?"

"I want you to tell me the truth, Lily. All I'm asking for is the truth."

"Is the truth going to change the situation right now, dad? I don't think so. No matter what I say right now it's not going to change anything."

"Are you sure about that, Lily? Are you sure we'll have Destiny as a client tomorrow?"

"Dad let me handle this. Trust me, we will still have Destiny Johnson as a client, that is not going to change. I know what I'm doing. Let us run through what we have and decide what we are going to tell her tomorrow before we go to Camelot and by this time tomorrow we will have our richest client to date and you dad will be thanking me for that."

Lily had been waiting in the dining room for five minutes before her phone rang.

It was her date, Michael.

She was glad he called, fearing that she was being stood up, not something that happens often to her, if ever.

But that feeling was short lived, because Michael was saying that he could not make it to their dinner appointment.

He claimed he was not feeling well, that it was best he stayed in and they will meet tomorrow for breakfast. He would arrive at the hotel at 7am, two hours before they needed to be at Camelot, so that they can have their meeting.

Although she didn't for a second believe that he was really sick, she agreed to the meet him tomorrow morning.

Lily hung up that phone, wondering what was really going on and if she would have to demand her money back from Michael and let him keep the information because she was not sure it was of any value anymore.

She had misread too many situations and people lately; the messes were piling up. Maybe it was time to turn her attention to saving the firm and its new client.

She needed Destiny Johnson as much as she needed her dad right now; to lose either one of them would be too great a loss and she cannot afford that.

Now that she almost certainly believes that John's plan is to take Destiny on his way out of the firm, she had to work harder at saving both.

Lily motioned for the waitress to come over, she was already there so she might as well eat. She was very hungry and pissed, some excellent food and wine should take of at least one of those.

While she ate and drank, she also made plans for the future.

After Destiny's money was safely ensconced in the firm's bank account earning interest for a while, Lily will open a sound investment portfolio for their client. The real estate market was doing pretty good lately, that is one viable investment option, they also can look at buying shares in some companies, the opportunities were as bountiful as the economy was good. But what was more important to Lily is that all of these business transactions will go through the firm, earning them even more money.

She planned on making Destiny Johnson the firm's number one client, and who knows, she may even come to like the woman as much as she liked her money.

She was also going to start looking for a replacement for John as soon as she got to back to the Turks and Caicos Islands.

Her dad hasn't told her as yet, but she was sure he intends to force John to resign, and after the way he'd used her, she had no problem with that decision.

She was thinking about hiring a female lawyer, but she quickly scratched that, she could already see the cat fights. Women don't like her much and she never understood why.

God forbid if she ever had to give them an order, they'd instantly take it personally, rolling their eyes and hissing, much like the receptionist, Mary already does when Lily is around.

Sometimes she wished her office had an entrance that didn't require her to pass Mary's desk every day, so she could avoid the forced pleasantries with her.

Hmm, maybe she could just get rid of her altogether when she takes over the firm, hire a pleasant young man to do her job with minimal annoyance.

Lily finished with dinner then headed upstairs to her suite to record her plans for the future into her laptop before she forgot.

She felt like the day had righted itself. It felt like she was in the victory lane, almost to the finish line, her opponents left in the dust behind her.

When she secures Destiny's money tomorrow, it will prove to everyone that she is more than capable of leading in the absence of Daniel Daly and that she deserves to be boss.

She has it all planned right down to her dad's retirement party. It was going to be big in every way because it was not just a retirement party, it's also a coming out party for her with their family, friends and colleagues in attendance.

They will celebrate her dad's retirement, his thirty years of distinguished service to the community of Providenciales, and for the roles he played on the various government boards helping to create laws that better serve the country.

During his career, her dad has worked alongside teachers at public schools to help create school programs and activities to motivate kids to think bigger than the environments that they came from, to try harder to improve their learning skills and to make a difference, whether it takes them to a trade school, community college or universities.

She will remind those gathered that Daniel Daly has above and beyond the call of duty to serve his adopted country well and that although he was retiring he was not deserting them.

After all the pomp and ceremony, which her dad rightly deserved, was concluded, then it would be Lily Daly-Shaw's moment to be presented to the community, her moment to shine.

D-DAY

M r. Daly was invaluable to me, but I cannot put all of my eggs in one basket.

My plan b was firmly in place, whether I needed it or not.

The night before I left Providenciales I knew I had to leave a trail for my family in case something happened to me. I'd left two sealed envelopes at my house, one for my daughter Anna and the other addressed to my sisters. I told Anna that if she had not heard from me in two days she had permission to open her envelope.

I can still see the scared look she gave me when she asked if I was in trouble.

I told her I wasn't, then laughed to further reassure her and chase that look out of her eyes.

Yet, even then I'd wondered if I was not walking into something potentially dangerous. Having access to so much money makes you question people, it also makes people act in ways they usually wouldn't act when they know you have access to that kind of money.

"You are going to be so happy to open that envelope one day," I said finally. Trying not to reveal too much just yet.

In the seal envelope to her I had made a duplicate copy of my winning lottery ticket and a letter. I told her that I'd won the UK lottery and that I'd gone to London with Mr. Daniel Daly and his daughter Lily to claim it. I left the name of the law firm in Providenciales, Daily Cramer and Shaw and the name of the hotel where we were staying in London along with their phone numbers.

I don't think she has opened the envelope as yet because I have been in contact with her every day since I arrived, and she knows that I'm safe.

In the letter to my sisters, I'd repeated much of the same information, except I told them that my dream had finally come through. They knew what dream that was. I wanted them to know that the better life I'd dreamt

114

of since we were kids had finally arrived, and that as sure as it had arrived for me, it had also arrived for them. This is sisterly love, we are sisters and we are in this together, having this dream come true so late in our lives. It felt like being given a second chance to live the life we've never had.

We are in our fifties, sixties and seventies, and life had finally definitely thrown us a lifeline and we are going to hold on to it together for dear life. But, if this trip doesn't end well, I wanted them to know that I gave it my all.

I prayed to God that if this envelope was opened one day and that letter read, I hope I would be the one reading it to them, on a cruise ship somewhere sailing in the Mediterranean Sea.

Time to get dressed, I was certain that my planning had been rock solid.

But first, let me check again to make sure I'd packed all of the relevant documents - lottery ticket, claim forms, passport, driver's license, bank account numbers and checkbook. Got it.

On the bed was my outfit for the day and all the accessories. A lovely fitted olive-green dress, gold hoop earring and watch, black leather bag and a taupe color four-and-a-half-inch stiletto from Zara.

For the next half hour, I painstakingly applied makeup just the way Anna showed me months ago. Today was picture day and I intended to put on the best face I possibly could when I was holding that over size check with my name on it.

I knew that in that moment I would have to guard against my nerves getting the best of me, thankfully my lawyer would be by my side, just as he's been ever since they arrived in London.

Daniel had gotten in a solid and restful eight hours in last night.

He felt rested and ready to take on the day.

After his meeting in the business center with Lily yesterday, he came to a solution. It was time for him to be a lawyer again, at least for another month.

He was sitting on the brink of greatness and there was no room for doubt or regrets. He reminded himself that he'd come to London for one thing and he was going to succeed at that.

He finally appreciated how big this was and how it could seal his fate in a very good way, so he had to show up today for Destiny and for the firm.

What he was about to do was not wrong, it was business. He had a reputation to protect and a client he was going to keep in his firm.

He knew he was not going to be telling the whole truth to Destiny, but he was going to make sure she knew that this was in her best interest. He did not come this far to lose a client; he and Lily had already agreed that they would stick together on this.

As for John, he was not going to be given any choice but to sign the resignation letter that Daniel had already typed up.

People behave badly when there is a lot of money involved, but this wasn't just about the money to Daniel, this was part of his legacy and he was not going to retire a loser. He was going out on top, victorious. He was about to gain the wealthiest client to Daily Cramer and Shaw, then retire in style one month later.

He was going to throw himself the biggest retirement party the island has ever seen, invite his close friends and colleagues, adversaries and politicians in the Turks and Caicos, making sure that the news media was also present when he makes his speech.

He has been working on that speech for a while now. It would outline his accomplishments in the legal profession, his work with the government to put draft and help laws in the territory, his community work and about his replacement at the firm.

He intends to pass the baton on to Lily by officially naming her, in front of the society's elite, as the new head and face of Daily Cramer and Shaw. Then he would tell them of this moment, how he and Lily had just signed on their richest client ever to the firm, they won't name names, they won't have to. The news would have already leaked by then and that's just fine by him.

Winning is what he does best, and he was ready to seal this deal.

He stepped into the elevator going and pressed the down button. It was time for breakfast with Destiny and Lily before they head off to Camelot.

BREAKFAST

Lily was the first one in the group to arrive for breakfast.
She was early because she had a meeting with Michael before the others arrived.

She chose a table for four, not that Michael would be sitting here when Destiny and her dad arrive, but she wanted him to think so.

As she waited, she poured herself a glass of orange juice and a cup of coffee.

This day was so important to her and she was excited to get on with it.

She will soon show her dad how dedicated and capable she is of keeping the firm running and managing clients with millions of dollars.

He was going to be very happy with the plans she had outlined last night on her laptop.

While Lily was basking in her glory, John was on his way to their hotel to crash their party.

He had come up with a plan of his own.

He had just as much damning information on Daly as Daly had on him, information that could lead to him changing the name on the law firm to Cramer Daily Shaw if they fought with him.

By now Lily may suspect that he was up to something, but they won't see this coming.

117

As she lowered her coffee, Michael appeared almost out of nowhere at the table, a small smile on his face.

"Hello Lily, you are like a breath of fresh air this morning. May I?" he said, indicating the chair across from her.

She put her cup down on the table, ignoring his comment, "You may sit."

He pulled out the chair and sat down, keeping his own face inscrutable as he tried to read hers.

He was ready to get this little chat over with, then walk out of here with the cash she had plopped onto his car seat without even waiting to find out if he was willing to go along with her harebrained scheme.

But Lily had her plans for that five thousand dollars she'd given to him.

When Michael sat down she figured he would be sitting in that chair for no more than three minutes, that's how long it would take for her to bring this meeting to a close and get that cash back into her possession.

She no longer wanted the information, she wanted her money back. What happened between her dad and Destiny was no longer important to her.

She zoomed in on him.

"I see you made a speedy recovery, Michael. What did it take, a prayer or medication?"

He gave a little of a smirk, "Both, a little of both helps."

She was giving off a vibe that made him wary, but he was ready for her. Two can play this game, he thought.

His smile widened.

"Lily, could you do me a favor and put that coffee cup between those beautiful lips one more time, please. I love the way you do that."

She humored him and took another sip; let him have his little fun before she burst his bubble.

But instead he helped her move the cup from her lips and to his, staring into her eyes.

When he lowered the cup, still holding onto her hands, he said, "You look very beautiful this morning." He brought her hands to his lips, placing soft kisses on them.

She drew closer to him, as though she wanted to kiss him and whispered, "You cannot seduce me Michael."

He was quick with a reply, "Are you sure about that?" He kept his eyes locked on hers for another few seconds, then they travelled down to her lips, his curving up in a smile that sent a jolt through her, making her weak to her knees. Thank God she was already sitting, she doesn't think those knees would have held her weight if she was standing.

He leaned in, while gently pulling her a little closer to him, and breathed in her breath, then he kissed her softly, stealing her breath and sense of time.

When he finally lifted his head, just inches away from her face he said, "Don't you ever ask me to seduce a woman again, unless it's you."

He smiled into her beautiful face, kissed her on the cheeks then got up and walked away with her five thousand pounds.

The elevator door opened and out walked Daniel.

He headed for the breakfast room.

"Lily darling, good morning are you ready to roll?" he said as he walked up to their table.

Daniel looked around for the coffee machine, not noticing the dazed expression on his daughter's face.

When he returned with the coffee and sat down, Lily had already collected herself.

"Good morning dad, how was your night? Got much sleep?"

"More than enough, my love, I feel like I've been born again, if that's possible." "So, are we still on the same page here?" she asked, diving right into it. "Are we ready to do what we have to do to win?"

"We are on the same page darling, no changes," he said.

"Good dad, because we are a team. Today we will not apologize or let feelings get in our way. We will be direct and firm and remember that this is business. We know what we are doing, and she needs to trust us."

"Lily," he said, looking up at her, "you don't have to preach to the teacher."

"You are right," she laughed, "for a minute there I forget where I learned all of this. Let's get some breakfast now, I'm hungry."

I walked into the breakfast room feeling like there were eyes everywhere staring at me.

It made me a bit anxious. I was hoping to see Mr. Daly before we got to breakfast so he could reassure me, but he wasn't waiting when I got down from my suite.

I tried to shake off the feeling of being watched, knowing that I was being a little paranoid. I walked over to a row of coffee machines that were laid out on tables along the side of the room, thinking that from that vantage point I would be able to safety scan the room for my lawyer.

I grabbed a cup then looked around at the endless array of choices, sighed, I was not in the mood to be confused right now, so I randomly picked a machine and pressed depressed the lever over the cup. Coffee poured out.

Done with that, I briefly scanned the room, but felt someone standing behind me so I started moving. Before I could make one more step, I was halted in my tracks by a familiar had at my waist, then someone whispered in my ear, "You smell beautiful."

I spun around quickly, forgetting the coffee in my hands, and saw my lawyer standing there, so close I could feel the heat of his body. He jumped back just a little, out of harm's way of the hot coffee slushing around in my cup.

My fears and anxiety melted away and I wanted nothing more than to embrace him. But before I could put thoughts into action, another face popped into my line vision. Lily Shaw.

Lily was glowing, a wide smile lighting and transforming her entire face so much it took me by surprised. What could have made Lily look so relaxed and happy?

I was even more taken aback when she actually spoke pleasantly to me, "Good morning Destiny, you must be super excited this morning, this is the day you've been waiting for. In just three hours, you will be richer than us."

She never let me answer, more like the Lily I was familiar with, moving with, "Come on let's go and sit, our table is over there." Nodding her head to the left.

"Let's all have breakfast," Mr. Daly chimed in.

We walked over to our table, where Mr. Daly pulled out a chair for me to sit.

I saw that a plate had already been fixed for me.

He saw me staring at it, "I knew you were coming, so I went ahead prepare it for you. I hope you don't mine."

"No, not at all," I replied.

He pulled out the chair to my left and sat down, while Lily took the one to his left. She was observing us, that unfamiliar expression still on her face. Was that joy?

That was really joy on her beautiful face, I mused, and I felt even more of my fears and anxiety dissipating.

We dug into our breakfast together, like a happy family of three.

I was feeling safe now that my lawyer was sitting next to me.

I wondered if I should mention the dozen pink carnations John had sent to me yesterday. What good would that do though?

I chose instead to just let it go and pretend it never happened as no one else knew about it, besides, mentioning it now would completely change the mood of this lovely breakfast.

It felt like John was trying to start something I was sure I did not want to be a part of, especially if it would cause problems between me and my lawyers.

It felt sneaky and underhanded and I was not going to be a party to any power plays between them.

Mr. Daly was quietly eating his food with such concentration I was sure he was not really tasting what he was putting into his mouth. Hmm, penny for those thoughts.

Lily kept the conversation, one-sided though it was. She was the happiest I have ever seen her in the last four days. I wished I could look be that at ease and happy right now.

One minute Lily was going on about the political situation in the United Kingdom, then changed the subject abruptly into her desire to head back to Turks and Caicos tomorrow instead of Thursday because of work.

I wasn't interested in what she had to say, not that she was looking from a response or acknowledgement, so I let her rattle on as I picked at my food, scanning the room.

I saw Michael sitting near the door, no doubt waiting on them to be ready, but he had such an intense expression on his face as he stared at Lily.

Hmm, I wonder what that's about. For all his good looks, Michael doesn't strike me as Lily's type, she seemed too haughty to ever consider a mere driver as a suitor.

Michael probably just has a schoolboy crush on her, I thought, dismissing him from my mind as I took a sip of coffee and tuned Lily back in for a minute. Lord, can she talk.

I looked down at my watch, needing to know how much longer we had before we had to leave for Camelot. I needed to reapply my lipstick, powder my nose and do some deep breathing exercises in the restroom to relax myself further before the big moment.

Raising my eyes from my watch, I felt compelled to glance over by Michael again. This time, he was not alone, a man was shaking his hand in greeting as if he knew him. Michael gestured over to our table in response to something the man asked.

The man turned and walked over to us. Is this who I think it is?

I nudged Mr. Daly so hard I knocked his elbow off of the table, "Look straight ahead," I whispered urgently to him.

Mr. Daly's voice boomed out as he pounded the table, making the dishes and utensils dance.

"For the love of god!"

Lily's head snapped back, as she fell silent, staring at her father in surprise. Then she followed our gaze to the incoming stranger.

Her beautiful face turning ugly as it twisted in contempt.

From their reactions, I knew who he was, and I knew that things were about to get unpleasant in a few seconds.

THE OTHER PARTNER

John Cramer did not ask if he could have a seat at the breakfast table. He pulled out the fourth chair at our table and plunked down into it, then proceeded to scrutinize us all, one by one. Staring at us with this piercing gaze as if he would decipher what each of us were thinking.

I am sure if one of us had opened our mouths, what came out would had been the same words, "Why are you here?"

But he beat us to it.

"Good morning Daly, Lily and let me guess this must be the lovely Destiny Johnson," he smiled at me, extending his hand in greeting, "I am…"

"No one cares who you are, John," Lily hissed, "Why are you here?"

John leaned back, pulling his hand back and folding them on the table when I didn't make a move to touch it, his smile widening as his eyes turned to light on Lily, "No need to be rude Lily." He paused.

"I can assure you I am not here to see you, believe that. Please let me finish introducing myself to our client."

He turned back to me, dismissing Lily, "I am John Cramer, senior partner in the law firm of Daly Cramer Shaw, and right now, all three of us are in your company. How about that?"

"We are all here because we have Your best interest at heart… or our very own, and we will find out which one in about ten minutes."

I'm guessing he must have practiced that opening statement he just made, it was so smoothly delivered.

I had no come back, because I was not expecting any of this, so I smiled slightly.

"Why are you here, John?" Mr. Daly came to my rescue.

123

"I am so glad you asked that question, because when I saw the look on your face and I heard your shout when I walked in, I wondered if you were having a spiritual awakening," John promptly replied.

Mr. Daly grunted annoyance, then said, "I am a bit surprised because I specifically told you that our meeting is at noon today not eight-thirty in the morning."

"I know, I know what time you summoned me to meet you Daly, but I had a change of plan," John said.

"Well, I did not have a change of plans," Mr. Daly shot back, "so I would like for you to dismiss yourself from the table."

"You are asking me to dismiss myself?" John laughed. "Now why would I want to do that?

"I think you are forgetting something Daly, I have just as much right to be here at this table as you and Lily. If there is a reason I should not be here maybe, it's time for you to explain."

I was listening keenly to what was transpiring in front me, wondering if John really thought he was going to Camelot with them, and if he was going to mention the dozen carnations he'd sent me yesterday.

If he did bring it up, I was going to deny receiving it, it's not like it was hand delivered. Then again, John looked like carnations were the last thing on his mind, he had bigger fish to fry.

Even though I knew a little about what was about to happen, the confrontation had taken me a little by surprise, and I wondered if I should excuse myself and let the partners deal with their issues on their own.

"Sorry John, but I would much rather you discuss your internal issues without me, I'll be in the restroom," I made to get up, certain I'd made the right choice to excuse myself.

"Sorry Destiny, but you can't go," he said, to my utter surprise. "The conversation we are about to have involves you, so, stay put." John said sternly.

"Excuse me?" I fairly shouted, certain that I had misheard. "I don't even know you."

"Well, I'm sure you are more than aware that I am a partner in his law firm," John replied, pointing towards Mr. Daly.

"What's makes you think I care," I shot back, my hackles rising.

"Well, maybe you do have a point there. Maybe you don't care who I am now, but after I explain my reasons for being here, you might not care for Daly or Lily either.

"So, please just give me ten minutes then you can make up your mind."

"We will not be giving you anything," Lily said. "You need to leave before I call security."

"Are you sure you want to do that, Lily?" John said, staring hard at her as if he knew something that would prevent her from carrying out her threat.

Mr. Daly put his hand on his daughter 's back and said, "Please, don't say another word, let me handle this."

He then looked at me, "Please do not believe a word this man says, he is only trying to save his own ass. I would also like to apologize to you ladies for having to do this in front of you, but John has forced my hand."

He then reached into his briefcase and pulled out an envelope, handed it over to John asking him to please open it.

John opened it and read the enclosed resignation letter, when he got to the end he was shaking his head in disbelief.

"Now sign it, here's a pen," Mr. Daly ordered.

"Well, well, "John tapped the letter, staring at Mr. Daly, "so, you are asking me to resign from the law firm. I can't say that I'm surprised by this, but I have one question."

"Really," Lily interrupted, "I would love to hear that question."

"You will as soon as you shut up," he replied, never taking his eyes off of Mr. Daly.

"Lily, please let me handle this," her father said.

"Where is the proof that this so-called office affair really happened?" John asked.

"Here is the proof," Mr. Daly reached into his briefcase again and came up with two photos. He placed them in the center of the table.

The color drained out of Lily's face. "Dad, where did you get those… photos," she stuttered out.

In stark contrast to her reaction, John was smiling, he did not seem the least bit surprised.

Lily was mortified, and her dad tried to comfort her, apologizing for doing this in front of everyone, but he felt he had no choice.

"Don't worry, darling," he told her, "this will put an end to everything. He will have to sign that resignation letter now. Just wait."

I tried to summon some pity for Lily's plight, I tried really hard, but none materialized.

It was not that I was glad she was being shamed in such a public way, it just felt a little good to see her tumbled from her high horse just a bit.

I know it was a little catty of me to feel that way, but she'd never tried to engender in me any feeling of goodwill towards her. Her constant animosity, with the exception of this morning - and even that seemed fake and over the top - had managed to scrub away any desire I harbored of us becoming friends.

I wanted to roll my eyes in annoyance at her conduct, both with the office affair and now this, but restrained myself.

John was watching Mr. Daly trying to comfort his distraught daughter, not feeling an ounce of regret.

He was ready to get on with this business, not sit here all day watching these two feel sorry for themselves. Those photos were no surprise to him, just evidence that would help him clarify his next question.

He could see the same lack of pity in Destiny's eyes, and he understood why – Destiny did not like Lily, and he was sure that Lily, not Destiny, had made sure of that.

Mr. Daly finally managed to calm Lily down a bit, turning back to John, "What are you waiting for, John? You have the proof you asked for, do you think that's not you in those photos?" He scoffed.

An unperturbed John kept smiling, and I waited with bated breath to hear his response, this was more excitement than I would ever imagine on a Monday morning.

"Daly," he drawled, "I am well aware that's me in the photos. I do not deny that, but I am not the one having a problem with your proof, I think you are."

"I am?" Mr. Daly said scornfully. "How do you figure that?"

"I think you are having problems with your eyesight, old boy," John said.

That made me smile. Nope, Mr. Daly did not have any problems with his eyesight, none that I was aware of, that is. I could testify to that in court, if necessary.

I stifled a naughty chuckle at that thought.

John continued, "I want you to look at those photos one more time and tell me how many people you see."

"What? What on earth are you trying to do, John?" Mr. Daly pointed down at the photographs. "I can see it's you and Lily in those photos, I do not have a problem with my eyesight."

"Thanks for answering my question Daly, thank you for confirming that it's Lily and I in those photos breaking the law firm's policy," John nodded, then, eyebrows raised, added, "Now may I see the letter that you sent to her, Lily Shaw asking her to resign?"

Oh, a lightbulb went off inside my head. I glanced over at the father daughter duo to see how they were taking this news. Mr. Daly eyes had widened in realization and Lily's face was screwed up in contempt. Her personality really shines through her beauty when she's angry, I thought.

Clearly, they didn't expect this, John was using his brilliant lawyerly tactic on them, and they were at a lost as how to deal with it.

I can only imagine that's why Mr. Daly had partnered up with him in the first place, his ability to see and understand things better than most people.

This was a lot to take in before going to Camelot. Yes, the puzzle pieces were really falling into place, but I was still unsure why I was unceremoniously ordered to sit through what was clearly an internal office matter.

I glanced around, feeling a little annoyed and very inconvenienced, then I noticed that Michael had moved closer to the table where he could be within earshot of everything that was happening.

I shook my head, wondering what else could go wrong this morning, the highlight of which should have been me collecting my lottery winnings, but it seemed like there was a contender for that slot.

Mr. Daly and Lily had finally taken their eyes off John and were now whispering into each other's ears.

They looked like two conspirators hatching a plan.

Suddenly, "Destiny, did you receive the flowers I sent you yesterday?" John broke the silence.

Mr. Daly's head snapped up from Lily's ear, "What?"

"What did you just say to Destiny?" he enquired as if I was incapable of speaking for myself.

"I was speaking to Destiny, not you Daly."

Mr. Daly ignored that remark, "Why would you be sending her flowers, John?"

"Let's see," John tilted his head to the left, folded his right hand under his chin as his long index finger tapped his right cheek, "because I can?"

"May I speak now," I interrupted, annoyed at being spoken for and about in this manner.

"Please do," John encouraged.

"Okay, thank you and yes, I did receive the bouquet of carnations you send me yesterday."

I felt no need to lie, and I did not intend to be interrogated about it. It appeared that I now had three lawyers, something I did not ask for, but I was willing to be polite about it, for now.

"Thank you very much John, they were lovely."

"You are welcome, and I am happy you liked them."

"I did. They were beautiful and unexpected."

"In what way were they unexpected?" John was quick to question.

What the hell is this? Am I on the witness stand or something?

"Well," I replied, glaring at him, "until this morning you and I had never met, and the little I know of you, I'd heard it…"

John did not let me finish, "…the little you know of me you heard it from those two?" he said, pointing at Mr. Daly and Lily.

"Well, whatever they told you must not have been very good," he said with a smile, leaving little doubt that he had seen and correctly interpreted my glare.

He was making me uncomfortable – he seemed too relaxed, the questions seemed too rehearsed, like they were part of his game.

But I was not prepared to play along with whatever little plot he had cooked up to get back at the Dalys.

"What I meant was that I heard um… I was told that John Cramer is a senior partner in Mr. Daly's law firm."

He leaned closer, eyes narrowing knowingly, "Are you sure that's all you were told?" as if he could read my mind and knew that I was lying.

"I am sure John, what more do I need to know about you?" I really wanted to get up from the table and leave this conversation, but John was not done with his little game of cat and mouse.

He had another bone to pick with his partners and he was going to use me to do it, but I was not about to serve up my lawyer to him.

Mr. Daily had not said much about John, only a little about the affair and the actions he intended to take, all of that was on the table already. What did John intend to achieve with his interrogation of me.

My lawyer and his daughter were just sitting there quietly, seemingly now prepared to choose their words carefully and not give John anything that could be used against them. The resignation letter John asked for concerning Lily never came, because there was and will be no such letter and John knew it.

It looked like John had turned the tables on him, he was not leaving the law firm.

The letter was now back in the envelope where John had shoved it back into without signing.

As the silence lengthened and John sit there smiling smugly at us. Lily made a grab for the photos, putting them into her purse.

"If you are not going to answer me, then I will be excusing myself," I was done with this little game. I stood up to leave, staring pointedly at John, daring him to order me one more time.

I was going to the restroom to freshen up before leaving for Camelot, get some fresh air far away from this table, and that was that. Let them try to stop me, they can sit here and trash out their problems on their own.

It was becoming apparent that I had stepped into the wrong law firm back in Providenciales two weeks ago.

Who are these people, and how can I get away from them for good?

I had absolutely no problem watching John stick it to Lily, she deserved it.

Those photographs were a definite hoot, not in a million years would I have imagined that much passion from a cold fish like Lily.

But enough about this little drama, Camelot awaits.

NOT FINISHED

J ohn was looking at Destiny's body as she stood up to leave the table.

He was beginning to understand Daily's fascination with her and why he kept her so close - there was a certain charm and sexiness to her.

Or, maybe it was knowing that she will soon possess ten million pounds that really heightened it for him.

"Destiny," he said, finally speaking up as she was about to push her chair further back to leave the table, "may I ask you one more question before you leave?"

He didn't wait for an answer. "Were you privy to any of the dirty details about me when old man Daly here spent those late nights in your hotel suite? Or were you two too busy doing other things?"

Now he paused, smiling widely at us. Mr. Daly looked like he was about to have a stroke.

"You might want to sit back down," he said to her, and pushed the chair closer to me.

I slowly lowered my body into it, mouth agape.

"Do you have something to say, Ms. Johnson? John enquired innocently, as if he didn't just suck all the oxygen out of the room with that series of questions.

I was so in shock, I barely managed to squeak out, "What?"

How the hell did he know about us? Did Mr. Daly tell him? That seem improbable. Does Lily know as well? Who are these people and why did I get so involved with them? I was inexplicably scared and nervous.

John was no longer fascinating now that he had turned his wrath on her.

Through the fog of fear, I heard a furious Mr. Daly finally intervene, "John, I need you to leave right now. You have said and done enough, leave."

John leaned forward a little and pushed back his chair from the table. I started to breathe again, he was finally leaving, and this nightmare was going to be over.

But John only sat back and crossed his legs and arms, getting even more comfortable, "No, no, Daly I have just gotten started and this time it's all about you."

Mr. Daly was afraid of where this was going to lead. This slime of a man was not going to stop until he destroyed him.

"Sorry Destiny," John said quietly, touching her hands, and trying to look sympathetic.

"I am not holding any of this against you. You are still our client, regardless. You just got caught up in this in another way and I only want to make it clear to Daly here that I know what he has done. He too has broken the rules and we are going to discuss it right now."

He sat back and turned to Mr. Daly, "I want you to know that you are no better than me." Wagging his fingers at him in disgust.

"You are a self-righteous bastard."

"Wait a minute now, John," Mr. Daly said placatingly, "I don't think this is the time or place for this, and furthermore I've never said that I was better than you."

"Yes, you did, Daly, many times and in your own way, "John was not about to stop, "like when you handed me that envelope and ordered me to sign that resignation letter. That tells me again, that you think you are better than me.

For years I longed to be like you, while you reminded me that you had morals and standards that you held high."

Daniel had to stop him before this little song and dance when any further, Destiny did not deserve this.

He knew that John was just trying to make him feel guilty, and he was succeeding. He was wrong, yes, he was wrong for getting involved with his client, but this was not the place for this discussion.

He had to put a stop to it right now.

"So, this charade is about who is a better man? "he asked, trying to reign in the situation and salvage what remained of the firm's integrity and keep their client.

Why couldn't John see what he was risking, what they were all risking, by having this discussion in front of the firm's biggest client.

Sure, he had managed to buy himself some more time at Daly Cramer and Shaw, a month at most until Daniel could figure out another way to remove him, but at what cost?

The man has no respect for me and he is disrespecting our client, while making a fool of himself. How could he insult Destiny that way by asking her such a vile question?

Whatever she did or may not have done in the privacy of her suite is none of his business. You don't shake down your client to get to your boss. What the hell has gotten into John?

"I am not a perfect man, John," Daniel said.

"I see you finally found that out, Daly, good for you," John smirked. "When did you realize this four days ago when you could not keep your pants up or keep your hands off our client?"

"What on earth are you talking about John?" Lily finally spoke up, "Why don't you just leave, we have places to be and you are not welcome."

"Shut up Lily," John replied.

"You know what John, I am tired of you speaking to me like that."

"And I am tired of you butting in when no one is speaking to you," John answered. "Does your dad need a lawyer now?"

"Listen John, I will not sit here and let you disrespect my dad just to settle a score."

"Really, Lily?" John shot back. "You want to sit here and pretend that you had no idea your daddy was shagging our client?"

"John, now you are just reaching, you have no proof of that," Lily said, but she wondered if he did. She glanced over at Michael, whom she only now noticed was sitting closer to their table, not by the door where he'd disappeared to after their little episode earlier.

The same driver whom she had asked to spy on them for her, the one who never told her what he found out, instead presumptuously kissing her and walking away with her money.

Destiny was talking now.

"Mr. John Cramer, have you lost your damn mind? How dare you come to this hotel this morning and try to destroy my day? You sat here, uninvited and unwelcome and proceeded to rip into all three of us.

"Lily may deserve some of it, but not on my time, or at my breakfast table. Mr. Daniel Daly is my lawyer, you are not, and I do not care if you do not resign, you are not invited here. This is my moment and what you're doing here, right now is madness."

"It's not madness," John said when she paused to draw a breath.

"Yes, it is, and please enlighten me how I am part of any of this," she said angrily.

"It's not madness, it's the truth," John replied, a little less cockily.

"Whose truth, Mr. Cramer, your truth? Who asked for your truth this morning? I sure didn't. I don't care to hear your truth, now please leave," she pointed to the door.

John did not budge, saying instead, "Destiny you need to know the truth about Daly and I'm going to tell you right now."

Daniel suddenly rose to his feet, he'd had enough of the morning's unwelcome entertainment.

He was not going to let him open his big mouth again. To think that this crude creature was still a lawyer in his law firm, disgusted him

He looked over at Lily and she was busy on her phone, hopefully seeking further advice on how to force John out of the firm.

Indeed, that is what Lily was doing. She was mortified that she had ever slept with this vile man at the table.

She is going to take him down; with a little more digging something will turn up on him that she can use to beat him. If he thought this little charade was going to deliver the boss's chair into his filthy paws, he had another thing coming.

She knew how he thought, he would use her father's own ethical nature against him. Now that he had fallen from grace, John would use that to beat her dad into submission so that he, not her, would be named the head of the firm when her dad retires.

That is a reality she cannot live with.

THE TRUTH

S till standing in front of his chair, Daniel motioned Michael over to the table.

Michael was asked to get the ready as they would be leaving for Camelot in ten minutes.

He was ignoring John as he gave these instructions. He had heard enough, and he was not going to sit here and be held hostage by him any longer.

If John needed someone to listen to his crap he knew a good shrink he can recommend. He was done with him today, he had an appointment that he had to make and right now that was more important.

He would swear John had lost his mind, and nothing he could say right now would make any difference.

While Daniel was fed up with the events of the morning, Michael on the other hand was intrigued at the little spectacle that had playing out in front of him for the past several minutes.

He'd finally put the pieces together as to Destiny's identity, he'd only heard bits and pieces of the conversation, but he'd caught the last bit about Camelot, and there could only be one reason they were going there.

As Michael left the breakfast room, three of the four occupants of the table gathered their belongings together, ready to follow him out.

John opened his mouth again.

"Destiny, I am going to tell you the truth," he repeated, "the whole truth, so help me god."

"I don't need your truth, John. You can go straight to hell," I shot back, dropping my cellular phone into my purse and picking up my sunglasses.

"Darling," John drawled, "that is exactly where you are heading with these two if you don't hear me out. You are walking into hell, you don't know them. They will eat you alive. Do you really think they are here because of you? You think if you were not holding a lottery ticket for ten million pounds old man Daly here would have been in your hotel suite shagging you, for the last three nights?"

I was fuming, the feeling was so overwhelming I could feel it escaping my ears, my nostrils and my eyes, I grabbed my purse off the table and swung it straight for John Cramer's face.

"You are a pig of a man, I wish to God I had never met you," I hissed at him as he rubbed his hand across his cheek, feeling for bruises.

Undeterred, he continued, "You don't think it was about love, now did you Destiny? I hope not, because my dear, you would be fooling yourself.

"You see in our world, Daily Cramer Shaw, winning comes first, in every sense of the word."

"Could someone please call security," Mr. Daly said, looking around for a waiter, anyone.

"Come on Daly," John said, "are you going to stand here and tell me that you did not sleep with our client. Yes or no? Let me hear you tell the truth because we all know the truth, even Lily."

"I have no proof of that," Lily shouted.

"Yes, you do Lily, "John said, wagging his finger at her, as if to say, 'naughty girl'.

"You knew what was happening and you wanted to stop it, but you couldn't."

A pissed off Lily repeated, "I have no proof of that."

But John clearly had all of the dirty details, "Lily, you wanted to stop it from happening so bad that you paid Michael five thousand pounds to seduce Ms. Johnson to keep her away from your dad."

A horrified Mr. Daly swung to stare accusingly at his daughter but willing her not to speak and give John anymore more ammunition.

"This is the truth the whole truth, Destiny, these are the people you trust. Lily needed someone to spy on you and her daddy while she spent the last three days with me," he centered all of his attention on me now.

"Yes, I do admit that Lily was with me for the last three days. I know that's not what she told you… Dad." John was rubbing it in. "Do you want to guess what lily and I was doing… Dad? John asked.

"Hmmm, probably not, but let me tell you nevertheless." He paused, watching Mr. Daly change colors, "I was doing the same thing to your daughter that you were doing to our client. I was lying to Lily and you were lying to Destiny. So, you see, you and I are a lot alike after all."

"I can't stand you any longer," Mr. Daily said through clenched teeth, apoplectic with rage.

"You wouldn't have to as soon as you answer my question. Or would you prefer me to ask Destiny here, or Michael. Now, now, if either of you here fail to answer I can play the tape for you."

I'd had enough, I couldn't hold my composure any longer. The tears began to fall.

No one spoke a word into the deafening silence.

Mr. Daly and Lily's faces looked like they were made out of granite, while I stood there running a faucet.

John was looking at me, waiting for me to say something but I couldn't. I continued to stare at my lawyer.

My heart was beating faster than usual, and I felt lightheaded. I sank back into the chair because it felt like I was to pass out.

I became aware of whispering and looked up. Mr. Daly and Lily whispering to each other and John now was on his phone.

I couldn't faint, I willed myself to get it together as my body tried to fold in on itself to hide me from the guilt that was wracking me. I hated every one of them right now.

I was beginning to angry again, at these people in front of me who were all the same. They were treacherous, and they deserved each other.

I felt like a fool for ever trusting any of them, and my anger redirected inwards.

I felt stupid for allowing myself to become dependent on them, for trusting in them more than I trusted in myself.

I knew this was a fault of mine, I tend to doubt myself, but this had to change, right here and right now.

But first I had to get rid of these tears, how embarrassing it must look, me blubbering here like a fool while these three snakes stand here and coldly plot, none even thinking to offer some comfort to their "best and richest" client, like they love to boast.

I had trusted Mr. Daly with the most intimate parts of my life, yet here he stood, looking no better than his daughter and her lover.

It was time for me to rescue myself.

I don't need them.

I am here, and they are here because of me. I have something they wanted.

I will not be bullied, belittled or fought over like a half-gnawed chicken bone among dogs.

My consciousness was back, and I felt stronger.

As they three of them stood there, still plotting, I was learning how to own my power.

This is not about them, this is about me, I silently lectured myself. Stop making it about them, I am deserving of what is about to happen to my life in one hour, I am deserving, and I am worthy. That is why I was chosen, not them.

I am no longer invisible, I am no longer on the outside looking in on life. I deserve to be where I am right now, and even though I was certain they did not care for any of my inner struggles, I was not going to let them steal whatever joy remained in this day. And there was joy, a lot of joy to come, so don't let them steal any more of it.

"Take back your power," I whispered. "Take it back now."

I knew it was the money that was bestowing this power and renewed self and confidence in me.

It was already changing my life for the better. I felt wiser and stronger.

I realized that everything I did from this point onwards was all that mattered.

I no longer had to or wanted to lean on these people or wait until they deigned to acknowledge that I was still at the table.

This was truly my moment, I was finally going to own it like a boss.

I sniffed haughtily, wiped the rest of my tears away with a silk handkerchief I'd pulled from my purse and stood up, pushing my chair back hard enough to catch their attention.

"Mr. Daly, Lily," I glanced at them in turn, ignoring the uninvited guest, "I'm leaving now. I am going to Camelot on my own. I no longer require your service, so as of this moment you are no longer representing me."

I turned to John, and in the same calm and composed voice said, "And you sir, can go straight to hell."

Shoulders erect, and head held high, I walked out of the hotel and breathed in the stiff London air, wishing for the refreshing Caribbean breeze, blue skies and restorative sun.

Michael held open the car door, his eyes pointed downwards.

I stepped in.

He already knew where I was going and why, but I told him anyway.

"Michael, take me to Camelot please."

CAMELOT

I walked into Camelot alone.

That was not my original plan, but there's a reason why it was always important to have a plan b. Maybe this was fate.

In spite of my newfound confidence, I felt a tinge of nervousness. I quickened my pace, trying to out walk it.

A man was standing by the door, smiling, hand outstretched as I drew closer.

"Welcome to Camelot, Ms. Destiny Johnson, we have been expecting you," he said, greeting me with a firm handshake and a pleasant smile.

"I am Mr. Jones the director of Camelot, and this is Dennis the secretary. Follow us please."

"Sure," I said, nodding with a smile at both men.

"I stepped into the room, "Wow, so this is real. I am finally here."

Mr. Jones who was standing next to me looked at me with a smile and nodded, "I am afraid it is, Ms. Johnson. This is real, you are at Camelot. Will anyone be joining you?"

"No," I said, "I am alone."

"Very well then, please take a seat," he said. "May I have your identifications and the winning lottery ticket, please?"

Mr. Jones was holding a scanning gadget that he quickly used to verify my ticket, then he chanted," Yes, yes, all set. Carry on."

I am not sure who he was talking to, but I didn't want to ask and come off as rude, so I sat quietly until he was finished.

He then showed me into another room, and over to an oval table with six chairs, five of them occupied. The occupants were waiting for me, all of them smiling as I walked into the room.

I took seat, trying to breathe normally.

Mr. Jones led the introductions, "To the left is Jackie and to your right is Marion, they are our assistants and they will be helping you with the

paperwork today. All the forms that you need to fill in are in front of you."
He pointed at them. "Okay, any questions?"

I shook my head and he replied, "Lovely." Like I had just said
something fabulous.

Suddenly he boomed out, "Listen up everyone: I have an announcement
to make. This is Destiny Johnson, our newest UK lottery winner. She won
ten million pounds, please let's all welcome her to the winning circle."

I was expecting handshakes, but everyone stood up and began clapping
and chanting, "Yeah, yeah, yeah, yeah," in a singsong.

My hands were sweaty, so I rubbed my hands together trying to massage
the moistness away. Wiping it on my dress would have been too obvious.

The smile on my face was frozen to one side like I was having a stroke,
as all eyes remained on me. There were people standing in the distance
applauding and taking photos.

I wished at that moment that Anna was here to hold my hand and help
me to remain cool, as she calls it, to tell me that I would be okay.

I didn't know if to cry, laugh or pass out, I had no idea how to handle
this moment. The events of the past couple of hours had robbed me of any
calm I may have been able to summon had I left that table when I first
wanted to and gone to the restroom to collect myself before this moment.

I tried to speak, say something to show you're not a total nitwit Destiny,
I urged myself, but I only felt like I was shrinking right before their eyes, as
they cheered louder and louder, drowning out words.

Before I could lose consciousness, Mr. Jones came over to me again,
grabbed my arm reassuring and returned my ID's.

He saw that I was struggling to take it all in, so he whispered in my ear,
"You can do this."

These words, spoken by a stranger, had carried me through to this
moment, and to hear them now spoken by a someone I'd only just met, I
felt calmness being restored to my body.

MY JOURNEY

The room had stopped spinning.

When the laughter died down, the forms were filled in and my name was printed on that over size check - Pay: DESTINY JOHNSON. Amount: TEN MILLION POUNDS - I thought of where I came from.

This moment had been set in motion some fifty years ago and I could not put it all into words even though they were asking me to try.

My little speech was tucked away in memory, longing to finally be told.

"This is the road to Destiny," I began slowly, looking around at faces that had gone silent when I finally spoke up. I focused on the one familiar face in the room full of strangers, Mr. Jones, my gaze drifting down from his kind eyes, gathering my thoughts.

"My most enduring image is of an eight-year-old girl. Even now, almost fifty years later, I can still see her.

"A girl who spends most of her time daydreaming and wishing her life was anything but what it was. This girl wanted normal things like most kids - she wanted more food because sometimes she went to sleep hungry, she wanted new shoes, ones that were actually in her size, not the ones two sizes too large that had to be stuffed with newspaper so her feet won't fall out, or shoes so small that it peeled the skin off her heel and made her feet cramp.

"She dreamt of wearing new clothes, not just hand-me-downs, but clothes that were bought just for her, clothes that fit. She always wondered what it felt like to rip a tag off of a new dress or pair of jeans. She always imagined the joy that other people felt when they did that.

"Oh, how she wanted her life to be better, so she dared to dream.

"She dreamt of having a bed to sleep on one day and not the cold concrete floor that left her body aching. She dreamt of learning new things even though she didn't know what those things were, but she never felt she could because she never understood what was being taught to her. The poor nutrition deprived her of energy and focus.

"In her dream world, things were different, they were better, and she ached for those things, simple though they may seem.

"She wondered what it would be like to live in a big home with electricity, running water, a refrigerator, a stove. To live in a house with a bathroom, a tub and a toilet, to have a normal life."

I paused, but I dared not raise my eyes from the second button of Mr. Jones shirt. I was holding on by a thread.

"By the age of sixteen, her dreams had not yet materialized, and she felt that the only thing that would have saved her would have been an education - to earn a diploma, or a degree and have it proudly displayed on the wall…

"…Well, that never happened, and she wondered if dreams ever died, because she was still dreaming."

I felt a rush of bravery, so I looked up and out at the small gathering. They were still paying attention, and I felt pride, pride in myself and in my story.

"To that little girl who is now a middle-aged woman, I say that dreams never die." I smiled, my first real one since walking into Camelot.

"I am here today because she kept me alive in dreams and possibility. She dared to dream of a world that was bigger than her own…

"… she dreamed until that world became our destiny."

END

ABOUT THE AUTHOR

Lady Bee was born in the tropical paradise of Providenciales, Turks and Caicos Islands in the sixties. At that time, TCI was just a tiny unknown British Territory with little more than dirt roads, abundant vegetation and amazingly beautiful beaches, but with a rich local culture and indescribable potential.

As a little girl growing up in Blue Hills with little in the way of entertainment, she soon developed a love of reading.

It was a love that endured through the years, one which led her to write her own book decades later. But it wasn't an easy road, those twenty years - juggling motherhood, a husband and her writing aspirations.

Even though her responsibilities to her family took precedence, through the years she made a concerted effort to dedicate a little bit of her time to jot down bits and pieces of what has now become 'Destiny's Journey'.

During these years, she spent a lot of time away from her native country, traveling the world and learning about other cultures.

Then in 2012 she returned to her native country. With time on her hands and a newfound freedom, she began writing prolifically, finally accomplishing her dream of completing her first book.

That book tells a tale of a young girl whose long-held dream finally comes through in her middle age, taking her on a perilous journey from the Caribbean to the United Kingdom.

Lady Bee currently enjoys a comfortable and relaxing life in the beautiful island of Providenciales, where she is still writing, reading and studying astrology. She also dedicates a big chunk of her time to visiting with her daughter at University in the UK.

44039273R00089

Printed in Poland
by Amazon Fulfillment
Poland Sp. z o.o., Wrocław